Love from Dad xxx

Edited by
Miriam Hodgson

Foreword by
Zoë Ball

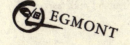
EGMONT

First published in Great Britain in 2002
by Egmont Books Limited
239 Kensington High Street
London W8 6SA

Contents

'We can't be raising those girls for all time! Look at how cats do. Raise up their kittens, wean them, don't know who the hell they are when they meet them in the alley a few months later. You think humans should be any different?'
Nat, father of four daughters, to his wife in Ladder of Years, *by Anne Tyler*

'I saw as clearly as one sees a mountain that he was the only man I've loved who loved me to the end, and never bruised my heart, and never for a single moment failed me.'
Pelagia of her father, Dr Iannis in Captain Corelli's Mandolin, *by Louis de Bernières*

Foreword

My dad first learnt of my arrival into the world whilst reading the story on *Playschool*: the crew held up cards saying, 'It's a girl!' behind the cameras. From that moment on, I was an out-and-out Daddy's Girl. There is no denying that Johnny Ball is my dad. I have been blessed with his big nose, silly grin and sticky out ears. It was to no one's surprise that I followed in his footsteps into a television career. Yet the similarities don't end there. Just like dad, I am a terrible timekeeper; I'm an appalling cook; I drive too fast; I'm often found serenading my family around the kitchen with songs of bygone days; I laugh at Bad Dad Gags; I'm never wrong and I always want to tell the funniest anecdote at the dinner table.

My teachers would agree that, sadly, I didn't inherit my dad's fascination with maths and science. But kids always rebel against their parents, and maybe that was my own little rebellion. Perhaps like my choice of. football team – my dad, a lifelong Liverpool FC supporter, had spent years trying to stir up some passion for footie in his tomboy daughter. When I finally found an interest in football (whilst living and working in Manchester), it was for Roy Keane, Lee Sharpe and Ryan Giggs. 'My daughter, a Manchester United Fan? Lasses have lost their inheritance over less.' He fell out with an ex-boyfriend of mine after an argument over Eric Cantona.

Sometimes I have been exasperated by the decisions my father has made; I've been frustrated at how overprotective he's been and angered by his high expectations of me. But as I grow older and have a family of my own, I am beginning to understand why my dad is the way he is. He has taught me that life should be lived to the full, to be honest, to love and laugh as much as possible. He still hugs me, muttering, 'I don't care what the others say about you, I think you're OK.' He'll kiss my head and say, 'And that's for nothing.'

I will never forget driving from Blackpool to London one hideous stormy night, when I was six years old. We broke down on the motorway and I was so scared. My dad wrapped me up in his big overcoat and as we waited for the breakdown services, he told me stories of The Billy Goats Gruff and sang me silly songs. I have never felt so safe from harm.

I love my dad and you know what . . . my dad loves me.

Zoë Ball

The Ship of Theseus

Anne Fine

'Careers advice!' Mr Lang's lip curled. 'I'll give you careers advice! Find out what you like doing most in all the world, and then look for someone who'll pay you to do it.' And I thought how, by that way of judging, my dad's in the right job. He's a philosopher. I couldn't even say the word when I was little. It came out as 'flossifer' and I hadn't the faintest idea what it meant, except I assumed it had something to do with that peculiar white stringy stuff they kept next to the toothpaste.

Not that he didn't keep trying to explain. 'I *think*,' he said. 'That's what I do for a living. *Think*.'

Mum's got no time for it. '*Thinking*, you call it? *Arguing*, more like,' she always corrects him, if she's listening. Because he doesn't seem to do it very quietly.

He's always thumping away about one thing or another, hoping that someone will pitch in and tell him he's wrong, so he can put them right about how he isn't. I'm like Mum. I act deaf – and stupid, too, if necessary – to get out of it. But Tabby listens.

Maybe she should be a philosopher too.

Strange thought. Because they're really weird, the things that it's his job to think about. Like when Tabs was little and splashing round in the bathtub while Dad was shaving, and she asked him suddenly, out of the blue: 'How do I know that all this round me isn't just a dream?'

He spun round so fast, so thrilled, he nicked himself quite badly. 'Look at her!' he called to Mum, blotting the blood from his chin. 'The philosopher's daughter! Four years old, and already an ontological sceptic!'

Whatever that is. And I must say, it does seem Tabby's far more on his wavelength than I am. I am forever walking into rooms to find the two of them wrangling away. Sometimes it's just normal family stuff, like her going on at him about finally finding the time to dismantle her stupid Squirrel's Night-time Hidey-hole halfway up the wall, so Mum can move in her new proper bed. (She is nearly *eleven*.) Or him grinding on about why tonight can't be the night they sleep under the stars. (She's been desperate to do this ever since I lent her *Oriole of the Outback*.) But Mum says she can only sleep outside if Dad is with her.

And he never gets round to it.

Too busy thinking.

This morning, it wasn't the bunk bed or the sleep-out. It was The Ship of Theseus.

Dad was explaining. 'So Theseus has this great big wooden ship, and everyone calls it The Ship of Theseus.'

'Makes sense,' I said. (I like to stick my oar in when I can – which isn't often.)

'And it gets more and more battered as time goes by – all his long voyages. So gradually, one by one, over the years, each single plank gets replaced. Every last one. And – this is the good bit – all the old planks just happen to float away in the very same direction, and fetch up, one by one, on the very same island.'

'Oh, very likely,' I scoffed. But Tabs was listening really hard.

'Now,' Dad said. 'On this island, it just so happens there's a master ship-builder, marooned for years. So he collects all the planks as they wash up on his beach, and one day, when he thinks he's got enough, sets to and builds himself a ship. And it so happens – pure coincidence, you understand – that every single rotting plank ends up in exactly its own place.'

He's grinning at Tabs now, and she's staring back, wide-eyed. It's obvious she can see something that I can't.

'*So*?' I say irritably.

Dad turns to me. 'What do you mean, "*So*?" It's only, put in a nutshell, one of the Great Central Questions of Western Philosophy!'

'What is?'

He stares at me as if I'm practically a halfwit. 'The *problem*, Perdita, is which is The Ship of Theseus?'

'Which?'

'Yes,' he says, trying to be patient. 'Is it the *old* one – I mean the one that's just been rebuilt from all the old planks? Or the new one that Theseus is sailing about in?'

I have to say, I take Mum's line on things like this. 'What does it matter?'

'What does it *matter*? Oh, it's only The Problem of Identity, isn't it?' He's clutching his hair now. 'Sweet heavens! It's only that awesome, overpowering question that's bothered some great philosophers their whole lives long: in what, exactly, is identity invested?' He's practically reeling round the room in his anguish.

Till he sees the look on Tabby's face.

She isn't even listening any more. She's lost in thought. Totally absorbed. Honestly, you'd think, to look at her, she could be Theseus on his firm new deck in a good wind, seeing, to his astonishment, a ship sail past, and wondering: 'Well, which one's mine? Neither? Both? This one? That one? But *why*? Perhaps that one first but, at a certain point, this one – or the other way round. But at which point? And why? Why? *Why*?'

The Philosopher's Daughter! So you can see why I spend so much of my Saturday out in the garden with Mum. We think that they're both daft. By coffee time, they were arguing about whether, if no one ever gets to see a particular tree in the middle of a forest, there's any way of being confident it's there at all. Then, later, as Tabs was setting the table for lunch, they reverted to the business of the sleep-out.

'Well why can't we do it *tonight*?'

'Not tonight, Tabitha. I have a lot of work to get through tomorrow. I'll need a clear head and a good night's sleep.'

'You're always saying that.'

'It's always true.'

Mum poked at the risotto. 'Oh, not the sleep-out argument. Not again, *please*.'

(No point my offering to be with Tabs. All Mum ever says is 'Better one daughter murdered than two.' And even Dad daren't argue.)

Tabby moved back to the bed business. 'Well, why can't Dad at least take down my Squirrel Hidey-hole, so I can get my new bed in?'

'It's not as easy as it looks,' Dad said. 'That little bunk bed of yours is a complicated structure. It'll take time to dismantle it.'

Tabs slammed the last of the knives and forks and spoons down in their places. 'Bed? I'm so big now, it's practically a *cage*.'

'I'd take it down for you,' I offered, to try to help her make Dad feel guilty. 'Except that you've had to sleep in it so long that some of the screw heads are so badly rusted I can't get them started.'

'Don't think I haven't wasted hours of my own life trying,' Mum said, to pile it on.

'All right!' said Dad. 'I give in! Straight after lunch I'll loosen the screws enough for Perds and Tabs to take the thing down.'

'Hurrah!' said Mum. 'At last! And now could you two switch to arguing about something entirely different – especially not the sleep-out.'

I was only away for a moment, fetching the salad bowl. But when I came back, they were already launched. 'Now look, Tabs.' Dad was saying irritably. 'Do try and pay attention. It's quite simple.' Grabbing the knives and forks and spoons she'd only just set in place, he built a sort of track across the table, and then divided it at the end. 'There. See the fork?'

'Which fork?' Tabs asked him.

Dad stabbed the place where his line of knives and forks and spoons split into separate directions. 'This fork here.'

Tabs told him, baffled, 'That's a *spoon*.'

(Honestly, sometimes I reckon, when people think too hard, all the blood must rush away to warm up the clever bits and not leave enough to keep the basics – that's just common sense – working at all. Mum says that's why these really clever people are always hours late, or wandering around lost, or striding about with their woollies unravelling behind them.)

'What he means is the fork in his road,' I explained. 'Not a *fork* fork.'

Now Tabs was ratty. 'Well, he should have *said*.'

Dad was outraged. 'I did say! I explained right at the start. "This is the problem of The Angels at The Fork".'

'We're supposed to be eating with those,' I reminded them.

But, of course, neither of them was even listening. Sometimes you'd never think that Dad was thirty-seven and Tabs was eleven. You'd think they were both *three*, and busy squabbling in some sandpit.

'Ready to go on?' Dad asked Tabs, all sarcastically. 'Well, there are two angels standing by this fork. They look exactly the same. So do the roads. But one leads off to heaven, and the other to hell. And, though the angels are identical, one always tells the truth, and one always lies.'

'Always?'

'Always.' He beamed. 'And you, of course, want to

get to heaven. But you can only ask one question. And all an angel can reply is "yes", or "no".'

'That's all?'

'That's all.' He spreads his hands in triumph. 'So, Tabitha, which question should you ask?'

He sat back, waiting. I would have said, 'You obviously know the answer. So you tell me.' But Tabs loves problems like these. Her forehead wrinkles up. Sometimes her fingers twitch as if she's working things through like a maths sum. Sometimes she stares into space. And sometimes she even mutters. I reckon if you saw her on a bus, thinking one through, you might easily reckon she was batty.

Even wrinkling and twitching and muttering didn't help her this time. It really stumped her, you could tell. She was still thinking about it even after Mum served up, and while she ate, and even while we washed up and Dad went to fetch the screwdriver and the oil to loosen the screws on her stupid little bunk bed.

She was still thinking as Dad pulled out the first screw. 'I could ask . . .' She broke off, shaking her head. 'No, that wouldn't work.'

'What?' I asked, holding the end up for Dad as he unscrewed the next bit.

'Well, I could ask . . .' Again she stopped, just as I handed her the next strut. 'No, I couldn't. Because I might be talking to the angel who lies.'

'Couldn't ask what?'

She didn't hear me. She was miles away. She didn't even notice each time I handed her a piece of the bunk bed to put on the heap in the corner by the door. And Dad was so taken up with the excitement of whether or not she'd get it right that he didn't notice he hadn't stopped working. He just kept handing me parts of the bunk bed, then got on with unscrewing the next bit.

Finally he couldn't bear it any longer.

'Give up?'

Neither could she.

'Yes. Give up.'

So, while I was stacking all the pieces of wood to take down to the bottom of the garden, he told her. 'You choose an angel, point up either of the roads, and ask the question: "If I were to ask the other angel if this is the road to heaven, would he say 'Yes'?"

She thought about it. You could actually see her working her way through it. And then her face cleared and she beamed the same way he does. 'Brilliant! Excellent! That is so clever!'

I didn't mean to say it. It just popped out.

'I don't get it.'

Dad shook his head at me. 'That's because you're not *thinking*.'

Tabs turned to explain. 'You see, if the angel's answer is "no", then the road you're pointing along has to be the road to heaven. And if the angel answers "yes", it's the road to hell.'

'But how do you *know*?'

'It's obvious,' said Dad. 'It stands to reason, when you come to *think*.'

Tabby was kinder. 'Look,' she explained as we carried the bits of bunk bed down the garden path to stack them out of the way behind the apple-tree. 'Suppose you just happened to ask the honest angel. She'd truthfully tell you the other angel was going to lie, so "yes" would mean "no" and "no" would mean "yes".'

I managed to think that bit through, though my brain was practically *aching*.

Then, 'Go on,' I said.

'And,' she said, her eyes gleaming just like Dad's, 'if you had happened to ask the angel who tells lies, then she'd have definitely made out that the other would have given you the wrong answer.'

'Ye-es,' I said, still trying to catch up.

'So, just like before, "yes" would have meant "no", and "no" would have meant "yes",' she said triumphantly.

'Aren't angels *he*?' I asked, trying to keep my end up. But she'd dumped her last armful, and set off back to the house. So I just stood there a while, thinking about it.

And then I thought some more.

* * *

And that's how it turned out that, when Dad got exasperated with all the noise ('Tabs with her music on far too loud, and you with all that mysterious banging in the garden – you're driving me crazy. Please, can't the two of you just go off to your beds and read quietly or something?') we were as good as gold.

We came back twenty minutes later, ready for bed.

'Goodnight, Dad.'

'Goodnight, Perdita.'

'Night, Dad.'

'Goodnight, Tabs.'

She waited in the doorway, grinning. 'Well? Aren't you coming?'

He looked up, mystified. 'Coming where?'

'Down the garden for the sleep-out.' She spreads her hands, innocent as an angel at a fork. 'You know Mum says I'm not allowed to sleep out without you.'

'But we're not doing that tonight.'

'You suggested it. You only just said, can't we go off to our beds?'

His voice was heartfelt. 'Yes, indeed I did!'

'Right then,' she said. 'I'm only doing what you said. And my bed's outside.'

'Nonsense. I saw your mother and the two of you pushing it into your room.'

'No, no.' She winked at me – the genius who made

all this possible, standing there inspecting the blisters on my thumbs. 'Perdita's put my Squirrel's Night-time Hidey-hole together again halfway up the apple-tree – every last plank in the same place. So, just like The Ship of Theseus, it's . . .'

She turned to me. After all, I'd done the work. I ought to be the one to crow it. 'Ta-*ra*! The Bed of Tabitha!'

Be fair. He knows when he's beaten, fair and square. He just trailed up to fetch his blankets and a candle or two, so he could keep working. In fact, I think he was delighted, really. Chuffed to bits.

There's more than one way of being a philosopher's daughter . . .

Safe Hands
Marilyn McLaughlin

'No, for the last time, no. You're too young to go haring off to Portrush on trains.'

Dad slapped his hand down hard on the table. Bang! It must be sore.

Everyone was going to Portrush on the train – a Saturday day trip, cheap return, end of season. I had to go, I just had to, because Roy Henderson was going and when my best friend Alannah told Him that I was going, He said that that was good, and that must mean Something.

I didn't speak to the parents for days. I am good at silent rage. It's a volcano inside me, simmering away, ready to explode, some day. You wouldn't know to look at me. They had no idea.

'Daydreaming again?'

I'd show them who was too young for things. I bought a sachet of hair colour – electric blue – the same as the guy me and Alannah saw down town, with the big buckled boots and the silver claws glittering on his fingers. Alannah said she knew how to do the colour. She's going to be a hairdresser, sorry, hair*stylist*, to the rich and famous.

She came round on supermarket night when the parents went out and we locked ourselves into the bathroom.

'Yeuch! It's black goo!'

'It's concentrated.'

'Have you done this before?'

'Lean over the bath and close your eyes.'

It was the moment of no return. I could feel the cold gloop ooze onto the top of my head, and Alannah's hands, in yellow kitchen gloves, massaging it in. It was *my* hair, I could do what I wanted with it, and next week I was going to get a tattoo – on my bottom – maybe. So there. And go to Portrush, just whenever I wanted – maybe.

Ring ring, ring-ring, riiiinnnngggg. The doorbell! I shot up straight.

'It's them, back early! No key!'

'Rinse!' Alannah said and shoved me back down over the bath, flicked on the shower, gave me the hand thing. I heard her going down the stairs, crossing the hall, slowly, to give me time.

Electric blue flooded the bath. How could so much blue have been in one tiny packet – brilliant, shocking, vibrating, in-your-face blue? What colour must my hair be? I heard the door open below. I heard voices, but whose? The first towel I tried turned a bright forget-me-not blue. I hid it far down behind the hot tank and tried another; wrapped it round tight and tucked it in. I was disguised as a normal, non-blue-haired person. You wouldn't know to look at me.

Alannah came thundering up the stairs, crashing into the bathroom.

'It was Roy Henderson.'

I sat down on the toilet in relief. Not the parents. Alannah gave me an envelope.

'It's from Him! It's for you! It's from Portrush!'

I nearly dropped it. I had gone pale, and interesting.

'I can't open it!'

'Yes you can, stupid. Do you want me to?'

No, I did not. It was my envelope. It was a card, and inside that a little coloured paper bag, folded nearly flat, and inside that was a necklace with a dolphin on it, and on the dolphin was my name. Carol.

'It's beautiful,' sighed Alannah.

I strung it round my neck.

'I'll never take it off.'

A key in the lock. This time it really was the parents, struggling in with forty million bulging plastic bags and wanting help. Me and Alannah went down stairs, smiling, innocent.

'Wait till you see what we got you! Stay out here till I have it ready.' Dad heaved a big parcel into the front room. 'Ready now,' he shouted. 'Come and see.' He had a big folded plastic thing on the coffee table. Alannah was standing right beside me, all eyes. This was going to be embarrassing.

He pulled a little cord on the plastic thing. 'Dah-dah!' as if there was something clever about it. There was a hiss and the plastic thing shivered, swelled, began to unfurl.

'It is . . .' Dad announced, as the last wrinkles fattened themselves up, and we could all see what it was, though some of us didn't believe our eyes. '. . . the last remaining, reduced-priced Self-Inflating Mickey Mouse Rubber Play Dinghy with Integral Safety Rope. For the beach!'

As if we thought it would be for anything else. It wobbled, settled on the coffee table, which it completely hid, so that it appeared, eerily, to float in mid air. It had a nose with whiskers at the front, and two big black ears sticking up. At the back there was a long black tail. That was the Integral Safety Rope.

'We'll try it out tomorrow,' said Dad, beaming, 'at

the beach – launch it. What do you think, girls?'

Nothing.

'Want to come too, Alannah? Plenty of room in the car.'

'No thanks.'

Me and Alannah went upstairs to dry my hair. It just looked dark and wet, but as Alannah, hairstylist, blow-dried, she said she could see a definite blue tone emerging.

'I wanted it really blue,' I said.

'It got washed off too soon. But you would still definitely know it was blue, and it will look even more blue by daylight, if you know to look for it.'

I looked first thing in the morning. Yes! By daylight, if you knew to look for it, my hair was definitely, slightly blue. Cool. I looked cool, especially with the little dolphin shining at my neck. Cool, blue, Carol of the hidden depths. It must mean Something, sending me a dolphin with my name on. Where was the card? I hadn't looked at the card! It was in the bathroom, still in its envelope. I read it.

See you tomorrow, outside the cinema, 9 pm please?

And there was His name, in His writing. This was the Something. My heart lurched, my volcano went out. Oh no! A real date! Not even Alannah had been on a real date. I couldn't go. I had to go. I couldn't go. He was the most fabulous creature in the universe, but I'd never spoken to Him on my own. I couldn't go. I couldn't not go.

'Breakfast!'

I went downstairs like a zombie. They didn't notice the blue hair. That was ok. My mind was elsewhere, up the Strand Road, after dark, on a date. I'd only ever been through town at night in the car, with Mum or Dad, watching the waves of people stream along the pavements, surge over the crossings. They were all so glamorous, confident. I didn't know how to be like that. I'd get tossed off my feet, carried away on the tide of them.

'It's only the Strand Road,' I told myself, 'that you go up every day.' But not at night, on a date, alone, in the dark – with the cinema lights all on, music banging out of the pubs, rows of barrel-shaped bouncers in white shirts outside the Trinity Hotel, people's faces red and purple from the neon lights, people drunk, people looking for a fight, fingers glinting with silver claws . . .

'I'm old enough, I've got blue hair, I've got a volcano within,' but I wasn't sure of any of that and the volcano had burned down very low.

'Come on,' Mum said, 'stop daydreaming, there's a picnic to be got ready.'

* * *

Someday I will not have to trek up the beach laden with picnic gear: rugs, biscuit tins full of sandwiches, Tupperware salads, Dettol diluted in a bottle, towels, swimsuits, warm coats because you never know when the weather will change, Mother's book, and Dad's terrible Self-Inflating Mickey Mouse Rubber Play Dinghy with Integral Safety Rope, still inflated because he couldn't get the air out.

They set off, cooing about the glorious day, the autumnal sunshine, the clear air, the fresh breeze, which chased goose pimples up and down my arms. The beach was empty but we still had to walk the whole length of it, to find exactly the right slope of sand-dune to camp on.

Dad wanted to go for a swim, at once, immediately. The tide was so far out it was only a thin dark blue line, out of earshot and almost out of sight. I hate swimming at low tide. It's too close to the bottomless deep, to sea monsters and slithery things.

'Come on, don't miss the fun.' That was Dad.

Mum had her sunglasses on, suncream on, bikini straps down and windbreak up. She was getting ready for her usual sleep, though she called it reading. Dad was on one foot with his towel held up by his teeth.

'Come on. Don't be a spoilsport.'

Then he was in his bathing trunks, doing his warm-up exercises.

'Race you to the water,' he said and off he went, looking silly, racing on his own. I drooped around for a little bit longer, just to make a point. Then I changed into my swimsuit.

'You'll want to take *that*,' Mum said, waving her book at it, 'or you'll be sent back for it.'

I jogged off after distant Dad, Mickey leering and bouncing along behind me, on the end of his Integral Safety Rope. It just wasn't fair. The sand hardened underfoot, and where it was ribbed by the waves caught the instep. Gnat-father on the horizon beckoned more madly, as if I was missing something, as if I'd be late for the sea. When I got there he was already waist-deep in the freezing water, diving into the big towering waves and letting them wash him shorewards in a clatter and splash of breaking surf. He roared over the clash of the waves,

'It's brilliant, come on in, get wet.'

I wouldn't let on, but the older I got, the more scared I was of the big crashing waves. I wanted to stay on the edge where the lacy rim of bubbles came and went. I wanted to stand just up to my ankles and not feel the pull of the glassy water back out to the deep.

'Come on in!'

He'd keep on until I gave up pretending I couldn't hear him. I left Mickey on the sand and waded out.

'Get down, get wet,' Dad shouted. I was jumping up

out of the way of the waves, to escape the chill. Nothing is as cold as the Atlantic swell on those big, open, Donegal beaches, especially at low tide. If you stay in too long your teeth chatter, you turn to ice. I dived into the next swell and rose up behind it, next to Dad. I shook the sea water out of my blue hair, tasted salt.

'Where'd you get the wee dolphin?' he asked.

I'd forgotten it was there. I put my hand up to it quickly, felt its small cold shape.

'A friend gave it me . . . just a friend . . . it's from Portrush.'

It was all right. I hadn't blushed. And I'd got in the bit about Portrush.

'Very nice,' he said and started counting the waves. Every seventh was supposed to be the biggest. We rose and sank on the swells as they passed. My feet left the ground with each one. I didn't like being loose in the water. I reached out my hand and felt Dad take it. His hand was chilled from the water, but it felt safe. We turned out to face the sea, the great long cold miles of it, all the way to America. We counted the waves.

'Four.'

The ground went out from under me, but my hand was locked tight in his.

'Five.'

'Turn before it hits you.'

'Six.'

'Don't let go of me.'

'Don't you want to fly?'

'Seven!' and he swings me round expertly into the lift of the wave and lets go of me. I rise dizzyingly on the big upwards roll of it, breathe in and then fly. I have forgotten how wonderful this is, the crash, the swoop of the surf, the strength of the sea under me, the softness of the bubbling water when I am finally left on the edge.

I snorted out sea water and blinked my eyes clear again, to see a leering Mickey Mouse dinghy surge past me, sucked out to sea on the back of the retreating wave. I lunged at it, missed, waded after it. The trailing black Integral Safety Rope whipped against my legs, snaked away again, but I caught it. The sea pulled strongly, the Integral Safety Rope slipped out of my frozen hands. A few more steps and I'd catch it again. I could just dive into the next wave and come up beside it. But Dad had me by the strap of my bathing suit, and then tight by the hand.

'Don't get out of your depth. Let it go.'

Me and Dad bobbed on the waves a while, watching Mickey's maiden voyage. His two round black ears were alert in the breeze and I knew he was leering out over the wide ocean, ready for anything, making for America.

'You could always get another one, I suppose,' I said, in case he minded losing Mickey.

'No . . . no point . . . We're both of us getting too old for that sort of a thing.'

'I'll go in,' I said. 'I'm frozen.'

I set off across the sand back to where Mum was a far away tiny dot, sleeping. I was at the icy stage of cold, feeling stiff and brittle. I slapped my arms across myself. There must be warmth in me somewhere. I ran.

Mum towelled my hair, so vigorously that it was all I could do to stay on my feet. Would she see the blue? She gave me a cup of hot tea. Dad arrived, slapped his wet hairy chest like a gorilla, grunted and hooted, irritatingly untroubled by the cold.

'Have a sandwich,' Mum said to me.

My hair was starting to dry, dark and sticky from the salt water. Just as well. You wouldn't know to look at me that it was blue. But it would need washing before I went out. *If* we were back on time. What time was it? Watches were always left in the car in case they got in the sea or were dropped in the sand. If we were late, there'd be no date. My volcano could smoulder for days about that.

'Is it time to go home yet?'

'Don't think so,' said Mum. 'There's a lot of picnic left.' She was prying open a Tupperware box. Time was passing too quickly and too slowly. I'd be home too late. I'd never be home.

'I've to go to the pictures tonight,' I blurted out.

'You never said!'

'I forgot.'

'Who are you going with?

'Just a friend . . . um . . .' If I said it was a boy they'd not let me go.

'We'll be home in plenty of time,' Dad said. 'We'll not leave your friend waiting.'

We stopped for ice creams in Carrigart, then drove on through Letterkenny, past the sunset, through the golden fields at Burt, past Burt Chapel where Mum and Dad got married, up the Branch Road. Home.

'Tons of time yet,' said Dad. 'You run on up and get ready.'

By the time I got downstairs Mum was on the sofa in her warm pyjamas with her book. Saturday night was special at home. She lit the coal fire, put her feet up, had a glass of wine. Then she and Dad and me sat up late and argued with the TV, talked back to the presenters, watched old recordings of *Morse*. I didn't want to go out into the dark, strange, glittering night. I wanted to stay here, bored, cozy. I dithered in the open door of the living room.

'Don't you look great?' said Dad. 'Where'd I put the car keys?'

'Have you done something to your hair?' said Mum, squinting over her reading glasses.

'Just washed it.'

'Have a good time,' she said.

There was an empty parking space just opposite the cinema. Dad pulled in.

'Look at that, five minutes early.' He grinned as if he had done something clever.

'We'll just sit here until your friend comes. Don't want you standing about on your own. Is it the same one gave you the wee dolphin? Anyone I know?'

I had to tell him, and if he said no, I was too young to see films with boys, I'd go home to the firelight and *Morse* and chocolates and Mum and Dad's boring conversation, and then I could stoke up the volcano and feel wrongly done by, but safe, on familiar ground. So I told him, and he didn't say 'You're too young to go haring off to films with boys.'

He went quiet and absent-mindedly picked up my hand and fiddled with my fingers as if he was checking that they worked properly. He used to do that when I was little.

'How are you getting home then? Will I collect you?'

'I'll walk home. With my friend.'

'And if you change your mind, phone?'

'Yes.'

'OK then, you hop out and go wait for your friend. But I'm staying here till you meet him. Just to see you're safely landed.'

Roy Henderson was already waiting. He had come early. I just hadn't seen Him in the crowds of people.

Saturday night streamed all round us. He took my hand.

'Like your dolphin.'

I turned to wave bye-bye to Dad. I could just make out his hand waving back inside the car, catching the lamplight.

PFSDD

Adèle Geras

As she walked home from school, Del wondered what she was going to say to her parents tonight. She'd never had anything difficult to deal with at school before, but the choosing of options for GCSE was going to cause trouble, she was quite sure of it. She'd made her mind up, though, and now it was just a matter of persuading them. Most parents wouldn't bat an eyelid. She sighed. Other people's mums and dads were not like hers. It was a problem she'd had to deal with for as long as she could remember.

They'd always been funny. There was the small matter, for instance, of her name. When she was born (both parents had versions of this story, and Del had put together a sort of fair copy from their accounts of what happened) she was called Delilah.

'I'm not having my daughter named after a Tom Jones song,' Dad told Mum.

'Don't be such an ignoramus,' said Mum to Dad. 'Delilah is the woman who reduced Samson's strength by cutting his hair off. She's in the Bible.'

'That figures,' said Dad sadly, giving in. Mum had spent her formative years reading books about Women's Liberation, and figures of Female Strength appealed to her. There was no way she would change her mind. Stubbornness was her middle name, Dad always said. Still, as soon as the baby was born, Dad had started calling her Del, and the habit had spread to Mum as well, almost without her noticing it. When Dad had pointed this out, Mum had sniffed and muttered something about Delilah being a bit of a mouthful really. That was something of a triumph for Dad.

'I'm back, Dad,' Del cried as she opened the front door. 'Where are you?'

'In here,' Dad's voice sounded a bit echoey, coming from the kitchen. Del followed the wonderful smells and found her father frying onions. He was wearing a PVC apron covered in flowers with cats peeking out from behind the petals.

'I'm just getting the sauce ready for tonight,' he said. 'Sit yourself down and help yourself to a brownie. I made a batch earlier.'

Del smiled as she bit into the delicious, chewy . . .

what was it? Cake? Biscuit? A bit of both really.

'I like these,' she said, with her mouth half full. 'Have you put extra bits of chocolate in?'

'That's right!' said Dad, adding fresh peeled tomatoes to his frying onions.

'Brilliant!' said Del. 'You could be on TV like that Jamie Oliver, I think.'

'But I'm not young and dishy,' Dad said. 'I don't know what sort of audience a redundant steel-worker the wrong side of forty is going to get.'

'It could be a heart-warming rags-to-riches story,' said Del. 'You've had such fun since you got made redundant, haven't you? Admit it!'

' 'Course I have! I love all this stuff,' said Dad. 'And don't think it was all easy, either. Some of my pals at the Works still think I'm barking. You should have heard them last week when I turned up at football with a plate of sausage rolls!'

Del laughed. Then she remembered her problem.

'Dad? Can I ask you something? I want to hear what you think before Mum gets home.'

'Shoot, kid,' said Dad as he added oregano and freshly-chopped basil leaves to the sauce. He often used American expressions. It started when Del was tiny, and he pretended to be a cowboy or a policeman for her amusement.

'I've got to choose my subjects for GCSE,' Del said,

'and I've decided that I want to do food technology and art instead of physics and geography. When I grow up, I want to be a nursery school teacher. What's Mum going to say?'

Dad came to sit down at the kitchen table opposite his daughter.

'It's your choice in the end, isn't it?' he said. 'And you've never been that good at physics, have you? I can't think why she'd object. I'll support you, don't worry.'

'You're a star, Dad,' said Del. 'I'll go into the lounge and start my homework before she gets here.'

'She said she wouldn't be late,' Dad said. 'You get cracking on your homework and I'll assemble the lasagne and put it in the oven ready for supper.'

Del looked around the lounge. Every wooden surface gleamed with polish she could still smell. There was a vase of fresh flowers on the table near the french windows, and she smiled. No one else's Dad knew how to arrange flowers. He'd taken a class in it, to pass the time after he'd been made redundant, and like most of the other domestic things he did, he turned out to be really gifted at it. Even Mum, who had very high standards, admitted that her husband did seem to have a talent at what was normally thought of as women's work.

Del picked up the Aran jersey lying on the sofa and pulled off her school jumper. Dad was a fantastic knitter as well, and she liked the things he'd made for her much better than any shop-bought garment.

'Yoo-hoo!' came a voice from the hall . . . Mum! Del thought: Oh, gosh, here goes! and began to wonder when would be a good moment to break the news? Maybe she'd say hello to Dad first and then come into the lounge . . . too late, the door was opening and there she was, all shoulder-pads and shiny jewellery and make-up that looked as fresh as it had this morning. She was still carrying her briefcase. She worked for an insurance company and was now quite a high-powered executive. Her briefcase was like a badge to show everyone how important she was.

'What a day!' she said, and sat down on the sofa. The armchairs were covered in dust-sheets because Dad was in the process of upholstering them. 'Your father is a jewel and a gem but I do wish he'd hurry up with those chairs. They're taking forever. Tell me some news from school to cheer me up. How are things?'

'Not bad,' Del said, and then burst out: 'We've had to tell them our options for next year. I want to give up physics and geography and do food technology and art. I want to be a nursery school teacher.'

'You cannot,' said Mum, 'be serious. Food

31

technology! Isn't that what we used to call domestic science? I do not believe what I'm hearing. Tell me I'm dreaming, Delilah.'

Del gulped. Mum (who preferred to be called Vicki, but that sounded funny to Del) only ever used her full name when she was seriously miffed. And right now she was more than miffed. She was apoplectic. Her face, which normally she would never allow to go red, was almost purple.

'How about a nice cup of tea?' said Dad, coming into the room just at that moment, carrying a loaded tray. He set it down on the table and smiled at his wife. She glowered back at him and said:

'Has she told you? What she intends to do? How she means to throw away every single career opportunity she's ever had? What did you say? I don't believe it. I really do not.'

Dad smiled at her and put on his most soothing voice.

'Keep your hair on, Vicki!' he said.

'Don't say that! I can't bear that expression and you know it! I don't know what's wrong with you, Dennis, and that's a fact. This is our daughter's whole future we're talking about here and all you can do is stand there like a lummox pouring tea out of your Crown Derby teapot! Pathetic! That's what it is . . . pathetic.'

'I know it's Del's future,' Dad said. He ignored the dig about the teapot and Del could see that his calm voice was making her mum even angrier. 'That's the whole point, Vicki. You must let the girl decide things for herself. There's nothing wrong with wanting to be a nursery-school teacher.'

'I wanted more for her!' Mum wailed. 'I wanted a dazzling career. I wanted travel. I wanted money. Even fame . . . not wiping snotty noses and dishing up shepherd's pie for the rest of her life.'

Del was astonished by what happened next. Her dad – her mild-mannered, never say boo to a goose father – stood up, and put the teapot down on the tray. He turned to his wife. The tone of his voice was quite different from anything Del had heard from him before. It was probably, she thought, the sort of voice he used to have when he was bossing big burly steelworkers around. He said:

'Del must do what she thinks best. We cannot all be nuclear physicists or work as translators for the United Nations.'

Mum gave as good as she got.

'Rubbish!' she said. 'Women can do whatever they want these days. She's cutting off her opportunities. I don't want her to end up as just as housewife.'

'Some people . . . some women . . . *just* want to be housewives. In any case, she might decide she wants to go back and do a degree after her children have grown up and left home. Have you thought of that? I'm considering it myself, to tell you the truth . . . Del won't be this age for ever. She'll leave home soon, and then I am going to branch out.'

'Don't change the subject!' said Mum. 'I will not let this pass. I will not have my only child go out into this amazingly competitive world without some decent qualifications.'

'May I say something?' Del asked. Her mother and father looked at her and nodded.

'I'd fail physics and things like that. I'm not clever in that way. But I might be really good at food technology and well . . . more practical subjects. I'm very good at art.'

Del's Mum snorted. That was the only word for it. She said, 'Art!' so scornfully that Del leaned away from her, to escape the blast of her fury.

'That's it!' said Dad. 'I've had about enough of this. You won't listen to reason, Vicki, so there's nothing to be done. I am going to have to take action.' He was now in full steelworks mode and his wife blinked at him. Who was this strange man who had suddenly materialised in her lounge? What had happened to the gentle, apron-wearing, knitting-needle wielding paragon she'd been living with for the past few years?

'Ha!' said Del's mum weakly. 'I intend to go up to

school and have some words with the Head about what I want for my daughter's future. I don't know what action you could possibly take.'

'I shall take action that befits a good trade-unionist, which is what I was for years. I shall go on strike.'

Del's mum laughed.

'How can you possibly go on strike, Dennis? What an old silly you are! In any case, I just have to send a fax now . . . the New York office has been on my conscience all morning. Del, your school problems will have to wait till I have the time to deal with them.'

She flounced out of the room. Del said:

'Thanks, Dad. It's good of you to stick up for me, but she's going to get her way, isn't she? I'm never going to be allowed to do what I want, am I?'

Dad sat down again and picked up the knitting bag that he kept beside the sofa. He took the wool and needles out and turned to the complicated cable pattern.

'Don't give it another thought, my love,' he said to Del. 'I promise you, by the time you have to tell them at school, your mother won't have a single objection left. I'm going to show her . . . just leave it to me.'

Del's best friend, Marsha, thought the whole idea of Del's dad going on strike was barmy. Del herself didn't like to admit it but she didn't understand how it was going to work either. She began to find out when she returned home on the Monday after what she still thought of as The Row.

She let herself in and called out as she always did:

'Dad? I'm home.'

'Hello, Del,' Dad sang out, and Del frowned. He was in the lounge. Someone was in there with him. Why wasn't he in the kitchen? Why were there no cooking smells? What was he doing? She went to look, and found him on the sofa, with his feet up, watching *Ready, Steady, Cook.*

'Why are you watching TV in the afternoon? You always say it's the beginning of the end if I want to do it . . . why aren't you in the kitchen?'

'You've forgotten. I'm on strike. I'm withdrawing my labour.'

'What about supper?' Del was starting to understand what her Dad being on strike might mean.

'What about it?' Dad smiled. 'She'll have to sort it herself.'

'She'll kill you.' Del grinned at the thought of her mother's reaction.

'No, she won't,' said Dad. 'She'll get pizza or Chinese. Tonight, anyway. She'll do her best to pretend that she can manage perfectly well. She won't give in easily. You know your mother.'

* * *

Del's mum dealt with the strike by pretending nothing at all peculiar was happening.

'Oh,' she said when she came in. 'I see you've decided that it's takeaway for us tonight. How super! What do you fancy: pizza or Chinese? Or maybe curry?'

Del looked at her Dad and smiled. He winked at her. When Mum went out to the phone to order supper, he said:

'She won't know what's hit her in a few days, mark my words. Your options are as good as decided. You can tell them up at school if you like.'

'So go on,' said Marsha on Friday, looking wistfully at Del's plate as her friend went on to finish every single chip. 'Tell me more.'

'I have to eat all my chips,' said Del, 'because we are not going to have any proper supper tonight or for the foreseeable future. We've been getting takeaway for four days and it's already boring. Not only that. The dishes are piled up in the sink, what few dishes there are, that is. The laundry basket is overflowing. The iron hasn't been taken out for days. It's great.'

'You could do some washing, couldn't you? And the dishes if it comes to it. I mean aren't you the one who wants to opt for all this food technology?'

'Course I can,' said Del. 'I could cook supper too. And I'm not bad at ironing, apart from shirts. But I won't.'

'Why not?'

'Del looked at her as scornfully as was possible with a mouthful of chips.

'Solidarity,' she said firmly. It was one of the first words she'd ever learned to say. 'You don't cross picket lines in a strike. And even though my dad hasn't got any picket lines, I'm solid with him . . . all the way.'

'What're you going to do when your school uniform gets all grotty?' Marsha asked.

'Mum'll give in,' said Del.

'How, can you be sure? Didn't you say Stubbornness was her middle name?'

'It is,' said Del. 'But Knowing Which Side Her Bread is Buttered is her first name. Wait and see. We'll win, Dad says, because we have Justice on our side.'

'Yeah, well,' said Marsha, 'hope you're right, that's all. Won't do me any good being seen around with you if you're wearing smelly clothes.'

'Anyone home?' said Mum as she opened the door. 'What a night! I'm soaked to the skin just coming up the drive from the car.'

She made her way into the lounge. Del and her dad were on the sofa. They'd been watching *The Simpsons* on television. There were beer cans round Dad's feet and Del had two empty packets of crisps scrunched up beside her. The waste-paper basket in the corner was overflowing. There were two cups with dregs of coffee in them growing mould on the mantelpiece and no one had bothered to draw the curtains.

'Enough!' said Mum, shouting suddenly. 'Have you seen yourselves? This house is a tip. You both look like inhabitants of Slobsville, and that shirt, Del, is a disgrace. The cuffs are black. Not grey. Black . . . I wouldn't be a bit surprised to find you had lice. This has got to stop. Now. I like a joke as much as the next person, but this isn't funny any longer. I shan't stand for it any more. I've made my mind up.'

'Are you going to do the dishes and the cooking then?' Del asked. 'There might be a few things still left in the freezer that you could microwave for tea.'

'Certainly not!' said Mum. 'Your father is going back to his normal routine as of tomorrow.'

'I will, too,' said Dad. 'But you know my demands. Del is to be allowed to do all the subjects she wants to do.'

'What about if she does some of the ones she wants to do, and just keeps on with a few of the things *I* think are important?' Mum sounded more normal now that some kind of negotiation was under way.

'No, sorry,' said Dad. 'It's all or nothing. It's Del's life, Vicki. And you can surely see now how important all these boring *domestic* things can be. If you're not academically inclined, that is . . . look how quickly things go pear-shaped if no one cleans up. Remember when the dustmen went on strike? People soon got their priorities sorted then. And . . .' His eyes gleamed. He knew that Mum was weakening so he hit her hard with the clincher, just when she was feeling at her lowest. Del could see why he'd been so good at negotiations when he was at the steelworks. He smiled at his wife and said:

'And of course I forgot to say that if you agree to our terms . . . because Del and I are in this together, shoulder to shoulder as it were . . . I will take us all out for a slap-up meal. There's a new Thai restaurant opened this week on Brandon Street they say is really good.'

Del held her breath and crossed her fingers.

'I give in,' said Mum. 'You win. I know when I'm beaten. And I certainly know when I'm hungry and I'm starving now.'

'Yesss!' said Dad, and punched the air. Del said:

'Thanks so much, Dad! I promise to work ever so hard. And thanks for agreeing, Mum. It'll be great, you'll see.'

'Hmm,' said Mum. 'I'm unconvinced I must say . . .'

'Don't start all that again,' said Dad. 'You don't stand a chance against the PFSDD.'

'What's that?' Del and her mother spoke at exactly the same time, and Dad grinned.

'Haven't you ever heard of it? The Popular Front for the Solidarity of Dads and Daughters!'

Even Mum couldn't help smiling.

The Most Wonderful Father in the World

Jacqueline Wilson

We've got the most wonderful father in the world. Don't groan. It's true. It really is.

There are the three of us: Laura and Mikey and me. I'm in the middle. So I'm Piggy. I am a bit plump, actually. I pretend I don't care. I chomp away on Mars Bars and Kit Kats and say, 'Who *wants* to look as thin as a pin like Posh Spice?' I do.

Laura looks a bit like her. She's always been the pretty one. I think she's probably Dad's favourite but he's always scrupulously fair and makes a fuss of all of us. But sometimes he chats quietly and seriously to Laura, asking her opinion on all sorts of stuff, treating her like an adult. It's as if he feels she's the clever one.

I'm the one who comes top at school and yet Dad

hardly ever asks about exams. He acts daft with me. But he never ever calls me Piggy like the others. He calls me Lady Penelope and he says I'm the most beautiful girl in the world. I know he's joking – but I like it all the same.

He plays games with Mikey, too. They play wrestling and Mikey always wins. Dad calls Mikey the World Champ and runs round with him on his shoulders, cheering at the top of his voice. Mikey was born prematurely and was in hospital for weeks, tiny and wizened. He's okay now but he gets ill a lot and he's always falling over and hurting himself. He's the smallest, skinniest kid at school. He'd lose a wrestling match with the average hamster, let alone a big bouncy bear of a guy like Dad.

Mum was ill when Mikey was born and she couldn't look after us. Dad wasn't working just then (he's an actor, not really famous, but he's been in a soap once and two adverts – we videoed them and I've watched them ten million times) so he took over. We all thought shopping was boring so we had takeaway pizza every single day and Dad let Laura and me wear our dressing-up clothes and Mum's high heels all the time. We took it in turns to look after Mikey. Laura and I mostly gave him his bottle (a messy job) and changed his nappy (much much messier) but Dad often gave him his bath. Mikey howled when Laura tried to wash him, his little old man's face red with rage, but when Dad held him and bobbed him up and down in the water and blew raspberries on his tummy, Mikey squealed with joy.

Mum got slowly slowly better and started doing things around the house in a slowly slowly sort of way, Mikey perched on her hip a little dolefully, not quite sure about this new parent in his life. He made it plain he wanted Dad more. We all did. But Dad had a new acting job – or he said he did. Anyway, he was out all day and a lot of the night too. Then one weekend we heard a lot of shouting long after midnight. It was Mum. Dad never ever shouted.

I got into Laura's bed and she hugged me tight and told me it would be all right in the morning. but when we got up and ran downstairs to look for Dad, he wasn't there. Mum was sitting at the kitchen table feeding Mikey. She wasn't concentrating on what she was doing. Mikey had finished his milk and was desperately sucking up air. He'd get the most terrible wind and cry for hours, but Mum looked as if she was past caring.

'Where's Dad?' I asked.

'He's gone.'

'Where?'

'Search me,' said Mum. 'I think he might have gone for good this time.'

He had gone. For *bad*.

We all cried. Mikey too, though he didn't know exactly what was going on. He just wanted Dad. We all did. Even Mum. Though she said she hated him.

'You girls think he's so wonderful. You don't know what he's really like. You just don't *know*.'

We did know, because Mum told us often enough over the next few years. She told us about Dad's lies and his broken promises and all his different girlfriends.

Laura used to put her hands over her ears and scream at Mum to shut up. She said Mum was the liar. So I did too. It made me feel a bit better blaming Mum. Though I often thought it might be *my* fault. Maybe Dad didn't want to stick around with a great big swotty piglet daughter. Maybe he'd been really happy when it was just him and Mum and his lovely Laura – but then I came along and skewed it all up, and then perhaps little Mikey was the last straw?

Laura told me much later that she'd always thought it might be *her* fault, because she was so ditzy at school and didn't always know the right things to say to Dad to impress him.

Last year when Mikey started school he burst into tears the first day because he didn't know how to fix his school tie.

'Dad left us because I'm such a wimp,' he sobbed.

'Rubbish,' said Mum. 'He went because – oh just *because*. Your dad isn't the type of guy who stays anywhere for long. But you've got George now. He'll teach you all about ties, Mikey.'

Laura and I looked at each other and made identical finger-down-the-throat gagging gestures. You've got it. George is our sort-of step dad. He moved in with us a few months ago. It looks like we're stuck with him now. He is the pits. We just don't get what my Mum sees in him. He is the exact opposite of our dad. Laura hates him. So I hate him too.

We expected him to hate us. We thought he'd be ever so strict with us, seeing as he's a policeman. He met Mum when we were burgled. The thieves made a lot of mess and took all sorts of stuff. Laura and I were terrified they'd taken the video of Dad or maybe the bangles he sent us from India last Christmas. We relaxed when we found them, no longer caring that the television and the CD player and Mum's gold necklace were missing. Mum was shattered though and this policeman was very comforting. He even called round the next day to see if she was all right and had managed to get the broken window fixed. We thought he was just being friendly. Ha. He was *far* too friendly. Before we knew where we were he and Mum started going out together.

They're not married. Mum says she's had enough of being married. But she acts like George's little wife all right, getting up before dawn to make him his breakfast when he's on early turn, leaping up to make him a drink the minute he gets in from work, carefully starching his horrible police shirts until they're crisp as cardboard. She overdoes it with the starch. I've seen George surreptitiously running a finger round inside his collar. There are red marks where they rub, but he doesn't complain. He's so *cheerful* all the time, whistling away in the bathroom, tapping his fingers on the table, laughing at stupid comedy shows on the telly. Mum laughs along with him.

We try hard to wipe that grin right off his big red face. Well, Laura and I do. Mikey isn't really one of us any more. He's always been a bit half-hearted in his George-baiting, probably because he's never really known Dad the way we do. He still *sees* our Dad – from time to time – but he sees boring old George every single day. He hangs out with him and likes to wear his stupid police helmet and he leans against George's legs when they watch TV together. Mikey laughs every time George does. He even sinks his chin in his chest and tries to make his giggle as gruff as George.

But Laura and I more than make up for Mikey's defection. Laura is ultra-inventively devious. She rarely goes for face-to-face confrontation. She often doesn't need to say a word. She just raises one eyebrow or rolls her eyes whenever George says anything. When he brushes past her she hunches her shoulders and screws up her face as if he's a walking rubbish bag. And I copy her, glance for glance, gesture for gesture.

George acts like he doesn't notice. He sighs from time to time but he doesn't tell us off.

'He's a gutless wimp,' Laura once said, fiercely. 'He must be a totally useless policeman. I bet he pats all the thieves and robbers on the head and lets them all go free.'

But when Laura stayed out till gone midnight with some of her friends from school, George was absolutely furious with her. Laura said he couldn't tell her off because he wasn't her father. George said he knew he wasn't her father but he still cared about her and worried and he particularly minded that Mum had been going crazy wondering what had happened. He said Laura mustn't ever be so thoughtless again.

Laura phoned up our dad the next day. Well, she left a message on his answerphone. Several messages. Dad was probably abroad or busy working on some TV programme. But after a few weeks Dad suddenly turned up on the doorstep looking incredible in a new leather jacket.

'You get dressed up in your glad rags too, Laura,' he said. 'We're going out clubbing.'

I've never seen Laura dress so fast. And then she was off, hanging on Dad's arm, her face shining, and there was nothing Mum and George could do about it. She didn't get back till gone two. I know because I sat up in bed waiting for her, wide awake.

I knew Mum and George were awake too because

every now and then I heard them whispering, and once Mum went downstairs and made cups of tea. I waited for a Big Row when Laura came tripping home – but it didn't happen.

Laura seemed disappointed.

'Guess what time I got in!' she said at breakfast the next morning.

'We know,' said Mum, wearily.

'So what are you going to do about it? I thought I was forbidden to stay out late,' said Laura, jutting her chin at George.

'You were with your dad,' said George. 'That's different.'

'It's ridiculous, though. Your dad just did it to cause trouble. Keeping you out till the small hours! And on a school night too,' said Mum.

'It's a one-off,' George said quietly.

And it was. We didn't see Dad for ages after that. He didn't even come on Laura's birthday. Or mine. He sent wonderful presents. Well, he was two weeks late with mine but I *knew* he wouldn't forget altogether. I wish he could have come, though. I wanted to tell him all about my new school. I'd got a special scholarship to this big girls' school. Laura teased me a lot about it and said I'd turn into a right posh-nosh and she fell about laughing at the old-fashioned school uniform. She said she thought schools like that were seriously sad. I said I didn't care what she thought. Though I did.

I was dead scared the first day. Mum told me not to be so silly.

'Oh come on, everyone's scared on their first day,' said George. 'Don't you worry though, Penny. I bet you'll make lots of friends and love every minute of it.'

Amazingly, George was right. I *do* love my new school. I haven't got *lots* of friends like Laura, but I'm in this comfy little gang: Holly and Liz and Rachel and me. We've got this brilliant form teacher, Mrs McKay, and though I got a bit stressed the first term because lots of the others had learnt stuff that I didn't have a clue about, I managed to catch up. More than that, actually. It sounds like boasting – Laura circles her head with her finger to make out I'm getting big-headed – but I was actually top of the whole class. That meant I got the form prize.

There was a proper Prize Day evening. Your parents come. Your mum . . . and your dad.

'I can't wait to come,' said Mum. 'I'll clap like crazy, you'll see.'

'So . . . it'll be just you coming, will it, Mum?' I asked.

Mum looked at George.

'Not me,' said George quickly. 'Penny will want her dad to come.'

'Well, obviously,' said Mum. 'But what are the chances of him turning up?'

'He will. He *will*!' I said, passionately.

I left messages on Dad's answerphone. I wrote him a letter. And postcards. And you'll never guess what – he sent me a huge box of chocolates with 'Congratulations, Lady Penelope' and twelve kisses on the card.

'Look!' I said triumphantly.

'He knows you're supposed to be on a diet,' said Mum. 'And he doesn't say he's going to come.'

'He WILL,' I said, cramming two chocolates in my mouth for comfort.

I got all dressed up in my carefully ironed school uniform. I was ready very early even though I knew Dad was never on time. The prize giving started at 7.30. I'd asked Dad to come and collect me at 6 o'clock so that we'd have heaps and heaps of time.

The clock started ticking by. Six. Half six. Quarter to seven.

Laura had been teasing me about being a big swotty snot-nose, but when she went out at seven to meet her friends at McDonald's she gave me a sudden hug.

'I don't think he's coming now, Pigs,' she whispered. 'You and Mum had better get cracking.'

'Not without Dad, I said. 'He *will* come.'

I said it through clenched teeth. I was clenching everything, willing him to come. But no one can ever make my dad do anything.

At ten past seven Mum shook her head.

'We'll have to go now, pet, or we'll be late.'

'I don't want to go without Dad,' I said. I had my face screwed up. I was trying not to cry.

'*I'll* come,' said Mikey. 'I can wear my grown-up suit and *pretend* to be Dad. Watch me walk like Dad.' Mikey puffed himself up, squaring his small shoulders, and started strutting round the room. 'See, I'll be Dad! I'll go and get my suit on.'

He made a run for the stairs, trying to leap them two steps at a time. He tripped halfway up and bounced back down, landing on his leg.

'Aaaaaaaah!' Mikey screamed.

'Oh Mikey,' said Mum, in tears herself. 'Oh no! Look at your poor leg! Oh darling. We'll have to cart you off to the hospital to get it seen to.'

'Nooooooo!' Mikey roared.

'Yes,' Mum insisted. 'Oh dear, look at the time! What am I going to do? The prize giving starts any second.'

I waited for Dad to knock at the front door to solve everything. But he didn't.

'I'll take Mikey to hospital. You take Penny to her prize giving and then come and find us when it's all over,' said George. 'You'll be fine with me, won't you, Mikey, my pal?'

Mikey *was* George's pal now, but only when he was well. When he got ill he reverted to a baby.

'No! No! I want my mummy! Mummy take me,'

Mikey screamed, locking his arms round Mum's neck.

George looked at me.

'Then I'll have to take you to your prize giving, Penny, like it or lump it.'

So I lumped it. We drove Mikey and Mum to the hospital and then George drove us to my school. He's a policeman so he obviously shouldn't break the law but I happen to know he broke the speed limit – and he left the car right outside school on a double yellow line.

'This is an emergency,' he said, and he made a little police siren sound under his breath.

The prize giving had already started and we couldn't push our way to the front where our allocated seats were. We had to stand at the back, waiting for my name to be called out. I craned my neck, looking where all my year were sitting with their parents at the front, wondering if Dad might have turned up after all.

I was still willing it so hard I missed my name being read out.

'Go on, Penny, it's you!' George whispered, giving me a gentle nudge.

I walked the length of the hall, my legs wobbling when all the heads started turning to look at me. When I got up onto the stage I saw there were three empty chairs in the front row.

He hadn't come.

I couldn't cry up on the stage. I smiled and shook the

Headteacher's hand and thanked her for the poetry book she gave me. Then I walked off the stage, all the way back to George.

'Well done,' he whispered.

He put his arm very lightly round me and gave me a quick hug. I always flinched away whenever he came near me. But this time I stayed still.

After the prize giving was over we were all served coffee and cake.

'We'd better get back to the hospital for Mikey and Mum,' I said, though it was chocolate cake with frosting.

'In just a minute. See your friends for five minutes first. Enjoy your moment of glory,' said George. 'And treat yourself to a big slice of cake too. Blow that diet.'

Holly and Liz and Rachel and their parents all clustered round congratulating me. I blushed like a fool but it felt good all the same.

'You must be very proud of your daughter,' said Holly's dad.

George smiled. 'Penny's not *my* daughter. Her own dad should have been here but sadly he got held up. Still, I'm as proud of her as if she *were* my daughter.'

Laura would have made intensive vomit-making gestures. I didn't. I didn't say anything back – but when we were in the car diving to the hospital (Mikey *had* broken his leg but he got bright blue plaster, which thrilled him to bits) I spoke into the silence.

'Thanks, George,' I said. And I meant it.

I don't want him to be like a step dad to me. I've got my dad. The most wonderful father in the world, no matter what. But I've got George too. And maybe that's okay after all.

Like Flying

Julie Bertagna

Run, run as fast as you can, you can't catch me . . .

They are moving on parallel lines. She is high on the hillside, racing towards their special place, running through sun-speckled trees, kicking up a crackle-storm of leaves. He shouts from the path below, wanting her to stop but she's too full of speed and song. It doesn't seem possible to stop, ever, when something stubs her foot, stone or root, and now she is falling, falling too fast. The world tumbles and she is inside a spin of flashing gold, green, blue; tree, earth, sky.

Catch me, Daddy, catch me, please –

* * *

There is a long, slow moment when she is completely alone in the spin of herself. Then his body breaks her tumble before she hits ground, a cushion of chest, arms, hands and the world is steady again.

He is angry-upset, one hand raised to smack, yet he stalls and gentles it to brush the leaves and earth from her hair, hands, knees, face.

'Did I fall from away up there? Did I, Daddy?'

The tree-studded slope. All those solid trunks she might have smashed into, her head cracking open like an egg.

'I told you to stop.' His breath is panic-hot on her face. 'You could have broken your neck.'

Her neck snapping like a twig. She knows the sound, feels it inside.

'But I'm all right. See, I am.'

He clasps her hand too tight, still not smiling, and she walks quietly beside him the rest of the way to their special place. She won't say a word about her banged elbow or the raw graze on the back of her hand. She won't whine or whimper about the gravel in her shoe, she'll be so good and brave, since she's given him such a fright. But later on, once they are at the red velvet armchair, their special place, once they are watching the planes roar overhead, then she will tell him something strange about her tumble.

When they get to the red chair, the Saturday morning jumbo to New York is ready and waiting at the end of the runway. It's a real beauty, one of their favourites. They settle themselves quickly in the chair, Marianne perching as usual on one of its collapsing arms. From their vantage point just beyond the runway they have the best possible view.

The jumbo roars into sudden movement. The noise and power is overwhelming. It seems impossible that such a mighty machine could ever leave the ground. Only a wire fence stands between them and that massive metal bird. What if it careers off the end of the runway and smashes through the fence, right into the field where they sit on the red velvet armchair?

'It won't fall on us, will it, Daddy? It won't – ' Marianne falters, unable to put her fear into words.

Dad pulls her onto his knee and his hug makes her safe again. As the plane rises above them he tells her his dream, the dream he's going to make real.

'One day we'll fly on that great beauty. You, me and Mum – we'll have the trip of a lifetime to New York. Just as soon as I've saved enough, that's what we'll do.'

Marianne can hardly wait. She wants to stretch out her arms, plane-shape, and pretend to fly but she can't let go of her daddy, not yet. As the jumbo's vast shadow passes over them she remembers there's a special thing she wants to tell him.

Just for a moment, deep in the heart of her fall, there was no fear or hurt at all. It had felt like flying.

It *was* still here, after all.

Marianne remembered the feeling of anticipation edged with dread every time she had come here as a child, wondering anxiously if the red velvet armchair would still be there, or if some tramp or an eagle-eyed rubbish collector had spied it and claimed it. She looked at her watch. Almost time. But did the jumbo to New York still fly on a Saturday morning? She had no idea – it had been years since she had come to see it. Marianne perched on the arm of the chair. She would wait and see.

As a child she had never seen how ridiculous it was – this lonesome red chair among a thin clump of bushes in the field next to the airport. So many things in life had seemed odd or mysterious back then – rainbows and hiccups, snail trails and spiderwebs, shoelaces and schoolties – not to mention a hundred pleasurable things like bubblegum and muddy shoes that, mystifyingly, annoyed the grown-up world.

The red velvet armchair had seemed no more extraordinary than any of these things – except that Dad, the most sensible and serious of grown-ups, had brought it here once upon a time, when he was a teenager.

He must have been about my age, thought Marianne.

The idea had just burst upon him, he had told her, when he spotted it dumped in a skip. He had dragged it all the way from the city, through the fields to this very spot among the bushes just beyond the runway fence, and had made it his secret refuge from the world, a planespotter's hideaway heaven, where he could watch the planes night and day, whenever he had the chance.

Dad still kept up the planespotting habit once he and Mum married, even though work and family life left him less and less time, over the years. As soon as she was old enough Marianne would trudge along with him and then it became not just his, but *their* special place. Armed with crisps and lemonade, they would get here early on a Saturday morning and settle down to watch plane after plane rise into the skies. It felt like the best seat at the most spectacular show on earth.

Now the armchair was pretty wrecked. Well past its best to start with, time and weather had done their worst. It was a lumpen, pulpy mush, its arms collapsed and the springs poking through once-plush red velvet. Still, it was here.

But Dad wasn't.

At last there was movement on the runway. Marianne screwed up her eyes against the sun and watched as a massive plane steered into position for take-off. She knew its shape, she knew its markings and tail pattern. The eleven-thirty jumbo to New York was about to fly.

The very last time she and Dad had been here together was early last summer – that rain sodden morning before school when Marianne had sneaked out of the house, so sick and nervous she had been unable to eat a mouthful. The red velvet armchair was the only place she could think of to go, to be alone, to escape what lay in front of her. She was sitting there, drenched by drizzle, the calming coolness of soft summer rain on her face, watching the planes, when all of a sudden Dad was there too.

'Come on now. I'll drive you to school.' He handed her the schoolbag she had dumped in the garden. He was drenched too.

'I'm not going.'

Marianne had been quite adamant. Then surprised by a rush of tears, suddenly wanted to sob like a baby, but didn't.

'Yes, you are,' he said firmly, gently. 'It's not such a big deal, Marianne. It's not a matter of life or death.' Dad smiled his tight, tense, fractured smile and sat down on the sodden arm of the chair. 'What's so awful about an exam?'

'Everything. It's physics and I just don't get physics. There's something wrong with my brain – everyone else in the class seems to understand it all, it's just me. I'm going to be a huge, big, embarrassing failure.'

'In whose eyes?'

'Everyone's.'

'Not in mine,' he said.

Marianne turned to stare at him. A plane began to scream along the runway towards them, its nose just lifting over Dad's head, but she hardly saw it.

'You're the very one whose always telling me to do my best, to give myself the best chance in life.'

He nodded. 'That's right. Do your best. That's all.' He flicked a raindrop off the end of her nose. 'What's the worst that can happen?'

'I get zero per cent. It's possible. It's scarily possible.'

'Well, in my eyes you get full marks just for trying.' Now his eyes met hers with a steadying, trusting look that she would remember. 'Listen, I don't care if you get zero per cent. What I care about is that you have the courage to walk into that exam hall and try. That's more important than an exam pass.'

'Really?'

'Really.'

The plane roared overhead, straining hard against the pull of the earth.

'That pilot saw us! He waved, I'm sure he did.'

Dad laughed. 'They've been seeing us for years. They understand, they're plane-lovers too. If they weren't up there I bet they'd be down here with us, watching.'

He stood up, felt the sodden seat of his trousers and groaned.

'I've got a business meeting at nine. Some impression I'll make!'

Marianne burst out laughing as he pulled her to her feet and gently but firmly steered her towards the car.

'Just say you had a little accident on the way.'

He sat outside the exam hall well past his nine o'clock appointment. Marianne kept glancing at the car as the exam papers were handed out. He was just a blurry shadow through dripping wet, steamed-up windows. He couldn't possibly make her out among the crowd in the exam hall but he sat there all the same, so that she could see him. Marianne never saw him go, just looked up halfway through a question and realised he wasn't there any more. By then, the horrible fear and nervy sickness had vanished and somehow she was coping. She wasn't doing very well, but she was trying her best. She might not even pass but at least she felt sure she wasn't going to score zero.

It didn't matter anyway. Dad had already given her the most important mark as she stepped out of the car. A+ for courage.

Now, a whole year later, she was back out here in the

red velvet armchair trying to hold on to that much-tattered scrap of courage.

The jumbo stood ready. Marianne settled herself deep in the chair. A take-off still seemed an almost supernatural feat. Each plane had to break the laws of nature and burst through the binds of gravity to soar high and free above the earth. It was a mighty triumph of courage and willpower.

I have to cope, Marianne told herself. I must try to be brave.

Dad was back home fighting a solitary life-or-death battle, and all anyone could do was be there and watch – except Marianne had decided that today she wasn't going to sit uselessly by his bedside, she would come here instead, to their special place. Dad would understand.

At first there had only been the dredging tiredness but they'd all put it down to overwork. He always worked such long, late hours. Then there was the illness that wouldn't go away. Test after test was followed by an operation that didn't work – just resulted in a kind of fading, as if he were gently tumbling away from them. Now this. A sudden fall into some place where he seemed to be on his own and there was nothing anyone else could do to help him.

He was dying. Now. Today. It seemed impossible. He wasn't even old.

The jumbo revved up power. When it seemed it could no longer contain such enormous energy it burst into movement and ripped along the runway. Marianne stared into the face of the plane until in an incredible act of will it passed the critical point, the point of no return, and rose into the sky.

It was a miracle, an everyday miracle. Magnificent and terrifying.

The jumbo roared directly overhead. Marianne stretched out her arms to mirror its shape and for a single instant the girl and the plane were parallel, body to body. Its massive power shook the armchair to its core, made every cell of her body quake. Now Marianne raised her hands and waved. She couldn't see anyone but somebody might look down and spot her here in the red velvet armchair. She imagined them strapped in their seats, willing the plane to rise up into the heavens, feeling themselves part of that vast struggle of forces.

All that precious human cargo casting off their little lives and earth chains for a great journey into the sky, to fly like air angels, fast and free.

Fathers Know
Best

Steve May

'Bye Mum.'

'Bye Mum.'

Leaning on the railing in the departure lounge, Hat and Tash waved to their mothers. Their mothers were sisters, so Hat and Tash were cousins. They were also best friends.

'Come on girls,' said Mr Harold Hope, Hat's dad. 'Let's beat the rush hour.'

The big old Humber Hawk whispered back along the motorway, and in the back Hat and Tash whispered about Hat's upcoming party: who they were going to invite, what was going to happen.

'I'll tell you what's going to happen,' called Hat's dad from the front seat.

'You shouldn't be listening,' said Hat.

Mr Harold Hope ignored her, went on: 'Three things always happen at a party.' Hat hunched her shoulders, and, scowled, and mouthed along with her dad: 'Something gets smashed, something gets stolen, and someone's sick.'

'Yuk,' said Tash.

'Not at my party,' said Hat.

'Well,' chuckled Mr Harold Hope, flashing his lights helpfully at a car that was going too fast, 'we'll see, won't we?'

'If we had a party I bet no one would come,' said Mr Tom Timms, Tash's father, wriggling into his big woolly pullover.

Harold Hope leaned close to the changing-room mirror, carefully parting and combing his sandy grey hair.

'Oh,' he said, 'I think parties are pretty easy to organise. I think it's important for young people to have a chance to let off steam.'

'I always worry about the damage,' said Mr Tom Timms, tying his shoe laces.

'There's always three things that happen at a party,' said Mr Harold Hope, spraying his armpits with Old Spice.

Mr Tom Timms braced himself.

'Something gets smashed, something gets stolen, and someone's sick.'

And Mr Harold Hope went on, outlining how he was going to make sure Hat's party went smoothly and enjoyably for all concerned.

'So long as you let young people know what your limits are, then there shouldn't be a problem. You know, I've never once had to raise my hand or my voice to Hat, because she knows where she stands.'

Mr Tom Timms stuffed his squash racket deep into his bag, along with his sweaty shirt and trainers.

'With Tash, I shout, she slams doors. We had a typical row tonight.'

'My dad, he's just so unreasonable,' Tash said, smoothing the blue powder into a paste in the bowl.

'Don't get it in my eyes,' warned Hat, screwing her face up and pulling the plastic cap tighter round her scalp.

'He kept asking me if I wanted a lift anywhere, and I said no I'll walk, and then Sophie phoned and I was watching TV so I was late, so I said to Dad can I have a lift, and he exploded. I told him, if he's going to be like that, I'm never going to ask him to do anything for me ever again.'

Hat, wincing as Tash slapped the first dollop of bleach on her head, said, 'I think your dad's OK.'

'No he's not, he's neurotic, he wants to know where I am every minute of the day, and he keeps saying he'll do things and then when I ask him to he gets all stressed.'

'He's better than my dad,' said Hat.

'Your dad, he's scary,' said Tash.

'No,' said Hat, shaking her head so the bleach slid, 'he's not really. So long as you know how to handle him.'

'Which is how?'

'Lie.'

The two dads pushed their way out of the changing rooms.

'The thing to do,' went on Mr Harold Hope, 'is to set your limits, and always do what you say you're going to do, whether it's a threat or a promise. That's why I have such a good relationship with Hat.'

Mr Tom Timms shook his head. 'It's like last night. I said no way was I giving her a lift home, so she rings at half ten, and asks for a lift, and what do you do? I said I'm no way coming to get you, I told you you weren't having a lift, and she says, all right, I'll walk through these streets full of addicts, rapists and murderers. I mean, what do you do?'

'And so you gave in?'

Mr Tom Timms nodded. 'I gave in, because I couldn't

stand sitting there worrying and imagining awful things. At least if I go and pick her up I know where she is.'

'You must never give in,' said Mr Harold Hope, shaking his head wisely. 'If you set a guideline, you've got to stick to it, otherwise your children won't respect you.'

'I don't care if she respects me, so long as she's safe.'

'That's another thing,' said Mr Harold Hope, clicking open the smooth lock of the Humber Hawk, and pausing by the door. 'You know,' he said, 'I may not have taught Hat much, but I have taught her two very important things.'

Mr Tom Timms knew what was coming, and steeled himself.

'I have taught my daughter,' went on Mr Harold Hope, 'how to punch, and how to throw. And I think any girl who knows those two things won't go far wrong in life.'

Mr Harold Hope stood in the living-room doorway, rubbing his hands and beaming.

'Haven't you gone yet?' demanded Hat.

'Just one moment,' said Mr Harold Hope, and pulled his Super 8 film camera out of his cycle satchel.

'I want this film to show your mother what a good time you had at your party while she was away in Greece enjoying herself.'

The camera whirred as Mr Harold Hope panned round the big room taking in the neat trestle-tables, the red and white checked cloths, the neat piles of crisps and snacks. He lingered on the 'bar' with its squash, fizzies, and ('for the older boys') a three litre plastic bottle of Farmer's Bitter Shandy. The vintage radiogram sat smugly with its ghostly green light and a stack of 60s LPs at the ready.

Mr Harold Hope clicked off the camera.

'All set and ready for action,' he said. 'Have a really, really good time, and I'll be back at midnight.'

'Are you driving?' Hat asked.

'Of course not, my dear. I'm playing skittles, and if I play skittles I have to have a pint, and you know what I think about drinking and driving.'

Hat pushed him out of the front door.

'And remember,' said Harold, fixing his cycle clips round his corduroy trouser ankles, 'don't panic, because however sensible you might be – '

'Three things always happen at a party!' the girls shouted back at him.

Mr Harold Hope pedalled off steadily down the path, whistling casually. As he passed the car port, he gave a friendly wave to the Humber.

'Not tonight, old girl,' he called. 'Be good.'

'Right,' said Hat to Tash, 'let's get this place sorted.'

Mr Tom Timms settled himself for a relaxing evening at home. No worries tonight. Wife away. Tash staying over at Hat's. Safe as houses.

'So,' he told himself, 'you're got absolutely no reason to be anxious or worry about anything.'

In half an hour, Hat's house was transformed. The girls had forced the old radiogram into the downstairs toilet. In its place, a band was busy setting up speakers and microphones, and tuning their instruments.

'I need a drink,' gasped Hat.

'Here,' said the lead singer, offering her a small cold bottle.

'What is it?'

'Cider with a dash.'

'Of vodka!' added the drummer.

Hat put her head back and gulped down the icy liquid.

Mr Harold Hope was having a very enjoyable evening. He was exactly one third of the way through his pint, and one third of the way through the skittles match, and he was doing very well, with two spare cheeses, and a total score to date of 20 points.

The moon was out, well nearly, and the air was warm enough. The drummer was playing bongo on the wooden decking. Tash sipped her drink, and ran her hand through her hair.

'You've got lovely hair,' the drummer said.

'About later,' Tash replied.

'It's fine by me,' said the young man.

The door clattered open.

Startled, Tash looked round.

A crumpled Hat stood in the doorway.

'I've had a bit of an accident,' Hat coughed.

Tash peered down at the rug, and winced.

'I know your dad taught you to throw, but not throw up.'

'It was an accident,' Hat whined, 'it just happened.'

'OK, OK,' said Tash, 'leave it to me.'

The band was pounding out some thrash number about death and annihilation.

Tash danced through the party with the rug.

The rug was stiff and awkward.

Hat trailed along behind.

'Careful, or the puke's going to dribble out.'

Tash staggered to the washing-machine, and forced the rug in through the round porthole.

'Are you sure this is going to work?' asked Hat.

'Sure,' said Tash, 'you can do twice as much as this.'

'OK, hang on then.'

Hat rushed off and came back with an armful of stuff.

'What's that?'

Hat fed the stuff into the washer.

'That's the four towels we got the dye on, and Mum's cocktail dress.'

'What happened to that?'

'I was going to wear it tonight, but I got spaghetti hoops on the necky sort of bit.'

At nine twenty six pm, Mr Harold Hope scored his first flopper of the night, and everyone applauded, even the other team.

The band were taking a break.

Out on the patio, the drummer was showing Tash some interesting constellations of stars up in the sky.

'They control your destiny, sort of, like, man,' he said.

'Hey, what's that noise?'

Tash skipped over to the utility room door.

The washing-machine. It was whirring, and then a roar, louder and faster, like a plane accelerating for take off. But then the roar turned into more of a groan, and there was a rhythmic clanking too.

Hat was standing over the machine, holding it to stop it bouncing.

'Do you think it's OK?' she said, doubtfully.

'Sure,' said Tash. 'It's just spinning.'

At which moment, there was a noise like a bag of nails let loose in a food mixer.

'No! No! No!' shouted Hat.

Through the washing-machine porthole, the girls could see the drum bounding and churning and banging.

'It's out of control!'

There were sparks and smoke sputtering at the bottom of the machine. Tash leapt for the power point. But before she got there, the porthole door flew open, and water gushed up and out onto the floor.

Mr Tom Timms finished his third cup of coffee. The house was very quiet, especially the phone. Mr Tom Timms was trying very hard to relax, but what was that noise? He ducked to the window and peeked out. No one. Mr Tom Timms went to make another cup of coffee.

'It looks worse than it is,' said Tash, mopping at the flood water.

'That's the last towel,' Hat said.

The parquet floor was covered with towels: red ones, blue ones, beach towels, hand towels. And still the water sopped up.

The band was getting louder.

Hat put her hands over her ears.

A boy staggered past, holding his stomach.

'Where are you going?'

'I need the bathroom.'

'Up the stairs, second on the left.'

At 10:01 pm, Mr Harold Hope celebrated his masterly performance in the skittles by treating himself to an extra half of best bitter, and a packet of pork scratchings.

'Da-a-a-a-ad,' Tash gasped into her mobile. 'We need some help here.'

'No way. No way in the world, I'm watching Cilla.'

'She's not on now.'

'I videoed her.'

'But it really is serious.'

'As I recall it, we agreed, you're never going to ask me to do anything for you ever again.'

'OK. I'll do it myself. It's only a washing-machine.'

Mr Tom Timms stiffened, his eyes narrowed.

'What about a washing-machine?'

'It's just blown up and everything's flooded and it's just hissing and crackling down by the electric cable . . .'

Kevin got to the top of the stairs, and lunged for the bathroom door.

It wasn't the bathroom. But by now it was too late. There was a churning and surging up in his gullet and –

* * *

'How long do you think it'll take you?'

Mr Tom Timms was squatting on all fours, peering at the smoking washer.

'I don't know, an hour?'

'Well, be as quick as you can. And don't you dare let anyone see you.'

'What do I do, hide if someone comes in?'

Tash thought for a moment. 'Tell them you're the maintenance man.'

Kevin wobbled past, holding his stomach.

'The blokes all seem so old,' said Mr Tom Timms.

'Not as old as you,' said his daughter, slipping back into the party.

Hat patted Mr Tom Timms on the shoulder. 'The lads from school, they're really just such little boys.'

And she disappeared too.

In The Dog and Slipper, Mr Harold Hope was talking to his skittles mates. They were surprised, that he had left his daughter home alone having a party. And he was telling them the three things that always happen.

Hat dashed up to Tash.

'What now?'

'We've got a problem. You know those two guys I met at the Death Wish Club?'

'They're about thirty, right?'

'Right, well they're here and I think they're on something. One just threatened Darren.'

'Can't Darren look after himself?'

'Come on, the guy's huge.'

'Ask him to leave.'

'I did, and he just growled at me.'

'Well,' said Tash, 'there's no law against growling, is there?'

Hat glanced back over her shoulder. 'Look, it's worse than that. When he growled, I punched him.'

'Did he go down?'

'No, I hurt my fist and now he's after me.'

Mr Tom Timms stood up and wriggled his shoulders.

The door flew open.

Tash.

'Finished,' he said.

'Not quite you haven't.'

Tash pulled her dad towards the living room. The music got louder and louder, pounding and pounding. Mr Tom Timms bawled:

'I'm not tough. Why not ring Hat's dad? He's the one with all the assertiveness and he never has to raise his voice.'

'No way, he'll go ballistic if he sees all this. Anyway, this big bloke,' Tash cast her eyes down. 'I don't know if I ought to tell you.'

Her father's eyes narrowed.

'Tell me what?'

'What he said, to me.'

'Go on, go on,' panted Mr Tom Timms, his fists clenching.

Tash glared up at her father.

'What he said he wanted to do to me.'

'Right,' said Mr Tom Timms, 'where is he?'

'Just get them to leave, don't make a fight or anything, you can think of something.'

The two young men flexed their necks like turkeys.

'We're not leaving.'

'You can't make us.'

Mr Tom Timms smiled a big smile, and spread his arms wide.

'Leave? I don't want you to leave. I want you to stay, because we're going to be doing something very exciting any minute now.'

And from behind his back he produced the prayer book.

Outside, the two young men loitered, kicking at stones.

'They're not singing.'

'They're not praying.'

'I bet there's no Sally Army band coming.'

'That old git, he fooled us.'

'Why don't we go back in and sort him out?'

'Hang on,' said the other, 'I've got a better idea.'

'Well,' said Mr Tom Timms, 'I suppose I might as well give you a lift home, now it's all over.'

'No way,' said Tash. 'It's Hat's birthday. I've got to stay with her and help clear up and celebrate and everything.'

The carport door gave easily to the screwdriver. Quickly the two dark shapes were inside the Humber, and the engine coughed and then purred.

The radiogram was back in position, the green light glowing smugly. The Farmer's Bitter Shandy, untouched, stood primly on the bar table. The nibble plates were neatly stacked.

'Where are all the towels?' Tash asked.

Hat shrugged. 'I've stuffed them in the airing cupboard.'

'Can I go now?' panted Mr Tom Timms, putting the last-armchair back into place.

'Are you still here?' snapped his daughter. 'Come on, it's ten to twelve. Get out, get out! And whatever you do, don't let Hat's dad see you. You'd better go the back way.'

Mr Tom Timms sighed, and headed for the door.

'Wow,' said Tash, 'I think we've done it.'

'Hang on,' said Hat, 'there's one more thing.'

She went to the mantlepiece, and looked at the ornaments.

She picked up a jug, a trophy for skittles won in 1976 by her father. She drew back her arm like a baseball fielder, and flung the vase into the big mock fireplace.

Smash!

Tash hissed, 'Why on earth did you do that?'

Hat snarled back, 'Come on, keep up to speed, dummy. Remember the groundrules. To keep Daddy happy.'

'Sick, stolen and – '

'Smashed, that's right.'

If Mr Tom Timms hadn't been so busy hauling himself over the garden fence into the back lane, he might have seen Mr Harold Hope's Humber burst out of the carport, and swing with a screech onto the road.

'I told you so,' beamed Mr Harold Hope, rubbing his hands, and then kneeling to pick up the shattered jug.

'And Lucy had something stolen,' added Hat quickly.

'Good, good, good,' replied her father, standing up with a bit of a creak. 'Nothing too valuable, I hope.'

'Oh, just a . . . doughnut.'

'Good. That only leaves one thing.'

* * *

Outside Hat's room, the floorboards creaked as Mr Harold Hope paced backwards and forwards.

'What's he doing?' Tash asked.

'Searching for sick. He won't rest until he finds it.'

'Can't we put him out of his misery, confess to the chunder on the carpet?'

'It's not the same, he likes to see it with his own eyes – '

There was a yell of triumphant laughter from across the hall.

The two girls went to the door and looked out.

'What on earth's the matter?' Hat called.

Her dad poked his head out of his bedroom door.

'It's all right,' he chuckled, 'I looked everywhere for the sick, all over the house, but do you know where I found it?'

The girls shook their heads.

'Right in the middle of my pillow. Goodnight!'

And chuckling happily, he closed the bedroom door.

Hat yawned.

'All in all, it turned out OK, didn't it?'

'I don't know, yet.'

Tash was standing at the window, peering out. Hat yawned again.

'I reckon I'll turn in now. How about you?'

Outside, a horn parped.

'You must be joking,' said Tash, pulling open the window.

* * *

'It's three in the morning here,' yawned Tash's mum.

'But I thought you'd like to know Tash's all right.'

'Yes, thank you. But Tash is a very sensible girl.'

'That's right,' agreed Tash's dad. 'She may be selfish and scheming, but you can trust her not to do anything stupid. Unlike that air-headed Hat. You should have seen the trouble she got herself into tonight.'

Hat was leaning out of the window.

'I thought you told me everything,' she grunted.

Hanging on to her hands was Tash, trying to get a footing on the shed roof.

'There's everything, and *everything*,' she hissed, and jumped.

'Yes,' Mr Tom Timms went on, 'whatever you say about Tash, at least she feels comfortable with us and she tells us the truth. Don't you think?'

But the line had gone dead.

Tash slid off the shed roof and fell on to the grass. She was up at once, and ran to the gate and through it. It clanked but she didn't care.

'I didn't think you'd come,' the boy on the motorbike said, stooping to kiss her.

'Never mind that,' she hissed, pulling away, 'where's the helmet?'

For some reason Mr Harold Hope couldn't sleep. So, he went downstairs and made a cup of tea. And then he realised. He'd been so bound up and wound up with his daughter's party, he hadn't checked the Humber in the carport.

'Tsk tsk,' he said to himself, 'I'd better go and say goodnight to the Duchess.'

As he shuffled down the path towards his carport, a motorcycle roared down the lane.

Noisy devils, he thought.

It's 5am. Mr Tom Timms is dreaming of a washing-machine running out of control. Inside it is his daughter, waving her hands and shouting.

Outside his bedroom, on the landing, the phone starts to ring . . .

Abigail's Gift
Stephen Potts

'That one.' Naomi pointed through the window, her long nails clicking on the glass. She was careful not leave a nose smudge as Abigail had done, beside and below where hers would have been. 'I wouldn't ride anything less.'

The bike hung in the shop window, as if its wheels disdained to touch the floor beside the other ordinary-mortal bikes. *Dragon* was emblazoned in fiery red letters on its glittery black frame. No wonder it wanted to fly.

The price tag was hard to read, as if it were embarrassed to say how much Naomi's birthday bike would cost. Abigail squinted. 'Three ninety-nine?' she ventured. It didn't sound right. Naomi snorted her what-a-stupid-sister-I've-got laugh. 'Three *hundred* and ninety-nine.' she said, like a teacher. 'Pounds.' Abigail shielded her eyes from the shop lights' glare and squinted again. There was something else on the price tag: a word in front of the numbers. *Only*, it said.

When she turned away Naomi had already gone on ahead, and Abigail found herself walking the rest of the way to school on her own, as usual. Naomi always found a way, or an excuse, to leave her behind, but Abigail didn't mind – it gave her more thinking time before lessons started and thinking had to stop.

All the kids around here have mountain bikes, or live on next-birthday promises of them. But this is Norwich. There are no mountains for hundreds of miles. The steepest climbs are the speed bumps on the estate: do they count as foothills?

All right – not all *the kids. Some of them, all boys, have BMXs even though they aren't cool any more. But at least they BMX on them, if that's what you call bouncing up and down the steps outside the bank.*

All I want is a bike. Two wheels, handlebars. A rack on the back and a wicker basket in front. A bell. I don't need zillions of gears or metal tube bits sticking out of the axles to stand on and do stunts. An ordinary bike, that's all.

She shook her head and stopped at the corner opposite the school. The lights showed a red man standing still. Cars and vans and lorries swished past. A red-brown tarmac strip in front of her had a stretched out bike painted white on it, like a warning: we'll flatten you if you cycle here.

You know, a bike. Not for mountains, or BMX-ing down the stairs, but for spoke-sparkling freewheels on a country lane; for a slalom weave along the dotted white lines of a deserted road; a legs-akimbo schuss through after-thunder puddles. Racing a big barking dog along the river path, a little yappy dog in the basket, spaniel ears streaming over the handlebars, like velvet handwarmers. Just a bike.

The light beeped and the red standing man turned into a green walking one. Abigail dawdled across the road to join the other tributary streams flooding into the turbulent child-lake of the playground.

Abigail nibbled at her homework on the same table, and in the same way, as she picked at her Sunday dinners. Maths and Brussels sprouts were equally unpalatable, and, it seemed, equally unavoidable. She bit her pencil and pondered. *Is there such a thing as an exam in Brussels sprouts? Or does it come under General Greens, along with cauliflower and broad beans and . . .* She jumped up and dashed to the serving hatch, behind which she could hear the last of the dishes being cleared away. She burst the hatch doors open and shouted through to her startled mother. 'Mum, Mum! I came top in cabbage today!'

Concentrate, Abby, she told herself, after her mother

closed the hatch with a silent, bemused smile. But she knew she couldn't, not until her father came home. He'd have his tea: a pizza, a can of beer, and what was left of the cake, in front of the TV, while Mum went out to her evening job at the supermarket. He'd be asleep in front of the news when she came back. But at least Abby would get to talk to him meanwhile, before tiredness took over and made him go quiet. It might be Naomi's birthday, but he was even later than usual today. That's why her homework was taking so long.

At last the familiar sounds intruded into her grapples with algebra. She scribbled down any old numbers in the answer spaces, closed her book, and listened to the overture. First came the thrum of car tyres, the handbrake ratchet and the tick of cooling engine. Then the door chorus from the car, the garage and the kitchen, and into the duet. Abigail listened intently.

'Hello, love. I'm sorry I'm so late. Roadworks again.'

'Hello, Dave.' A pause for hugging. 'I've got to dash or I'll be late. I've left lasagne in the fridge, and there's salad needs eating up.'

'Thanks.' The fridge door, open and shut, a coda to the chorus. 'The bike looks good in the garage. All shiny. She must have cleaned it after riding it in this rain.' Abigail remembered how Naomi's face had fallen that morning when she found that her birthday bike wasn't the *Dragon*.

Another pause, but not for hugs. 'She's not ridden it. Dave. She won't.'

'Oh?' Hiss of beer can. Her dad had left for work early as always, hours before they were up.

'Mandy Cotterill's got one just the same. Naomi won't do anything she's already done.'

Car keys slammed onto the worktop. 'For God's sake, Alison.'

'I know, Dave, I know. She'll come round though. Just give her time.'

'Time? A whole weekend's *over*time I worked to buy that bike – and she'll not sit on it? Where is she, anyway?'

'Tennis class. Please don't be angry when she gets back.'

Another hug. 'All right. But when I think of all the interest I could have paid off, instead of buying that bike . . .'

The sheets flapped wildly in the blustery wind. Abigail grabbed an elusive corner before it escaped, and took the clothes peg her mother handed over.

'Mum?'

'Mmmmm?' came the peg-in-mouth reply.

'What's interest?'

A telephone rang inside the house. 'Hold on, love. I'd better get that. Your dad's having his first lie-in for months.' She passed the laundry basket to Abigail and ran for the kitchen: but the ringing stopped before she got there. Naomi yelled up the stairs. 'Dad! It's for you.' The only answer was a groan.

When she'd hung up all the washing, Abigail avoided the kitchen because of the raised voices within. She made instead for the garage, where Naomi's bike still wore its birthday bow. She lifted it away from the wall, enjoying its lightness. It may not be a dragon, but it was pretty fancy all the same. She swung her leg over the crossbar and lowered herself onto the just-too-high seat. She was about to set off up the drive when Naomi burst in and grabbed the handlebars.

'Don't you dare!' she hissed, like a puncture.

'Bikes are for riding,' said Abigail, twisting the front wheel from side to side.

'This is *my* bike: mine to ride or not ride.' Naomi stepped in front and gripped the wheel with her knees, as tightly as the wheel-grabber racks in the bike shed at school.

A shadow fell across the open door, cutting short any further argument. Their father had dressed quickly, and stubble flecked his cheeks. He looked awful. 'Sorry girls. No swimming after all. There's a problem at work and I've got to go.' The car alarm beeped.

Abigail jumped off the bike. 'Can I come too?' she asked.

Her father paused a moment before a smile cracked his tired face. 'Why not? If they call me in on a weekend like this, they can't complain, can they? Jump in.'

Abigail did exactly that, clicked her seat belt on, and grinned broadly at her cycle-rack sister as the car reversed up the drive.

'Dad?' she asked, as they bumped down the kerb and onto the road. 'What's interest?' He stalled the car. There was a pause, ending in a deep Dad sigh.

'It's what makes us work when we don't want to, Abby.'

When the car door opened, Abby saw relief written all over the face of the man in the suit. 'Sorry to call you in, Dave,' he said. He didn't sound it. 'But the system's crashed and we can't get it up. There's a lot riding on this, if you can get us back on-line by three.'

Her father got out of the car. 'Meet my daughter, Abigail. You don't mind?'

'No, no, of course not. We've always valued family life here at Harper's.'

'Hello, mister,' said Abigail.

'Mister Robson,' said her father. 'Mister Alan Robson. My boss.' He didn't look anything like the way Abigail had pictured him.

'Hello Mister-Alan-Robson-my-dad's-boss.' She held out her hand. 'What's interest?'

Mr Robson glanced at her father, who shrugged his shoulders, as if to force an answer. Robson hesitated, but not for long.

'It . . . it's one of the iron laws of economics, my girl. Let's say you want something: I lend you the money. When you pay me back you owe a bit extra. The extra's the interest.' He waved at the building behind them, as her father walked towards the big glass door. 'This business is built on it.' Her father stepped inside. 'So is your house.'

Abigail twirled round and round on one of the hundreds of empty office chairs, then reached behind to pull the lever that let her down with a hiss. 'So this is where you work?'

'Mmm-hmmm.' Her father's fingers flickered over the keyboard as he frowned at the screen. 'One of the places.'

'It's big. And empty. Why's no one else here?'

'Most of them work ordinary hours. But the machines don't get weekends off, and I have to fix them if they get sick.' He stood up and stretched. 'Abby, love, that squeaking chair and your chatter stops me thinking straight. See that light in the corner? That's my boss's office. If you go and talk to him a while I reckon I can sort this out and we can go home.'

Abby stopped twirling and set off in her chair, wheeling

past rows and rows of little cubby-holes with empty desks and blank computer screens. She stopped here and there to take in the little personal touches people had applied. A stuffed fluffy crocodile. Photographs. A miniature football, with names on. A model car.

'Hello Mister-Alan-Robson-my-dad's-boss.' she said as she rolled herself into his room. Everyone else just had a place – a *workstation*, they called it – but he had an office, with walls made of glass, so he could watch everybody. He didn't want her there, she could tell.

'It's not very interesting, is it?'

'What?'

'Interest. Why do they call it that?'

'I don't know . . . er . . . Annabel.'

She spun her chair, and said part of her name each time she faced him. It took three turns. 'A–bi–gail.' She stopped abruptly. 'How much would it cost for a day off? For my dad?'

'What?' he frowned.

'For him not to do this, for just one day?'

The blank screen on his desk sparkled into life. Numbers and colours flashed all over it. He jumped up. 'Brilliant!' he shouted, and made for the door.

Abigail's chair somehow blocked his way. She looked up. 'A day off. How much?'

'He's priceless, love.' He tried to dodge past her. 'You couldn't afford it.'

The chair's back rest suddenly collapsed, to block the door completely. 'I know he's priceless. That's why I'm asking you.' Behind her all the blank screens in the huge building came to life, illuminating teddy bears and baby pictures and pop-girl calendars.

'A hundred,' he said.

'Shake.' They shook hands, and Abigail wheeled her chair aside.

Abigail watched Naomi counting her money at the till. 'I haven't enough,' she said.

Abigail shrugged. It was always like this when Naomi waited for her on the way home. 'Put some back, then.'

'Can't you lend me? You never buy anything.'

'I'm saving up for something special.'

'So you've got plenty to lend, then.'

Abigail paused and thought. The time between Naomi's birthday and her own, another month away yet, was just enough: but only if she didn't spend or lend a single penny of her pocket money. Unless . . . 'Only if I get more back.' she said.

'Eh?'

'It's called interest.'

The newsagent laughed. 'That's right, love. A proper little businesswoman.'

Naomi scowled at them both while trying to decide whether to put back a magazine or some sweets.

'Some sister you are,' she said as they left the shop. Abigail ignored her and went into the bike shop next door. Naomi was puzzled: she watched through the window a while as Abigail pointed at bikes and chatted with the bike man. When she started trying them out Naomi spun on her heels and strode off.

'But will you ride it?' asked her mother, as she scribbled a note.

'It won't stay in the garage, Mum, I promise.' Abigail's fingers were crossed behind her back.

Her mother stuck the note under a Wallace and Gromit fridge magnet, next to the notes from yesterday and the day before. 'Make sure your dad sees that, would you, love?' She put her coat on. 'And don't say anything yet about having a bike for your birthday. It's best if I talk to him first.'

'OK, Mum.' Abigail closed the door and returned to her tea. She flicked through the magazine Naomi had left on the breakfast bar on her way out to tennis. It had been so long since they had all sat down as a family for an ordinary meal. Sunday dinner, with its Brussels sprouts torture, didn't count.

In the dining-room, the other side of the hatch, her homework lay in waiting, sprawled across the table like a silent paper monster, determined to tie her up with squiggles and batter her senseless with numbers. Abigail looked around. She needed a weapon. The best she could do was a large wooden spoon, with a big saucepan lid as a shield. She put the radio on loud to confuse the Maths Monster, slipped off her shoes, and crept out of the kitchen and up the hall to the dining-room door. She paused, took a big breath, and burst through, yelling, 'Your number's up now!' and then 'Crunch this!' as she battered the maths book with the spoon. They fought back vigorously, but her saucepan shield held firm and, after an epic struggle, she stood above the vanquished texts, breathless and beaming. 'And let that be a lesson to you!' she shouted at the geography books that still lurked in her satchel.

The radio clicked off, and gales of laughter blew through the open hatch from the kitchen. 'Spot of bother with your homework?' asked her father, between splutters.

'What a weirdo!' screeched Naomi. Abigail's face flushed scarlet as she closed the hatch.

The bike stood in the early morning hall, as she knew it would. There was a big bow on the handlebars and a small one on the saddle. It didn't have a wicker basket but it did have a bell. Abigail ran her hands over the dark green frame, so cold to the touch. She twirled a pedal, then spun the front wheel, enjoying the smooth whirr of the bearings and the new tyre smell. She sighed deeply, then crept back to bed, but she knew she wouldn't sleep.

Her Dad trudged into the kitchen and laid down his briefcase with a sigh, as if it weighed a ton. He was surprised to see Abigail there. 'Your new bike's not in the garage, love. I thought you'd be out on it.'

Abigail tried to smile when she shook her head. It had been so hard not to ride the beautiful bike. Her father looked around the kitchen, from Abigail, to her mother, to Naomi. None of them spoke. He frowned. 'Oh no, come on. Don't tell me. Not again.' Anger and weariness competed in his rising voice, till Abigail's mother shushed him.

'Abby's got something to tell you, Dave.'

'I didn't want the bike for my birthday, Dad.' He frowned again but said nothing, and sat by the breakfast bar. 'Well I did, but there was something I wanted more. I asked the bike man just to borrow it for a day, as long as I promised not to ride it. I paid him my pocket money for interest, and when I took it back I got the bike man to ring up your work. We talked to Mister-Alan-Robson-your-boss and he said yes.'

'Said yes to what?'

Abigail took the stool next to his. 'What I want for my birthday is for you to have a day off. And that's what we've got, now the bike's gone back. You can lie in as long as you like tomorrow. It's a half day at school, so you and Mum can meet us after and we can all go to the park. I want to go out in a boat. Naomi said she would row but I want a pedal boat. It's a bit like a bike but on water.'

Abigail's mum and dad gazed at each other. Her mum's eyes moistened and her dad looked away. Abigail thought she heard him sniff. Then a broad beaming smile spread slowly across his tired face, lighting it up like she hadn't seen for a long time. He swept her up in his arms and spun her round the room. Naomi dodged her twirling feet as she slipped out of the door.

'Yes, love,' he said. 'Yes. And then we'll go to the pictures, and come back here for a big dinner, all together.' He put her down and kissed her.

Her mum laughed at Abigail's questioning stare. 'With no Brussels sprouts. Promise.'

There was a knock on the window. Naomi stood beside her bike on the drive. She patted the seat and beckoned. Abigail shot through the door with a whoop of joy, not noticing the way her parents embraced behind her as she jumped onto the seat and raced off up the drive, Naomi trotting alongside.

The Hawthorn Shawl

Elinor Hodgson

Patience was low down in the hierarchy of angels, although her mother, Rimmia, was an archangel. She did not know her father.

Dancing in the asteroid belt one night, Rimmia had been caught in a meteor shower and unintentionally hitched a ride. Her rocky chariot propelled her through the Earth's atmosphere and dropped her, winded and dishevelled, in a silent clearing in the depths of the forest of dreams. Looking up at the stars, she smiled in wonder at their beauty. She wanted to watch them move across the sky as the planet revolved, but the peace and the heady smell of earth and bracken swept an immense tiredness over her and she spiralled into unconsciousness.

Cloaked by the night and the intertwined pines, Narjilu, the centaur and guardian of the forest, gazed on Rimmia in equal wonder. He had seen her fall amongst the glittering stardust and emerge from the blaze of light, a semi-human form, not unlike his own crossbreed, but with a power and grace he had never seen in an earthbound creature.

Narjilu watched over her for some time. Eventually he approached her, his hooves gliding over the moss and bracken like skates. He covered her shoulders in a hawthorn shawl – protection from icy splinters and Caron, the nightmare bearer. Even in sleep the glow of her skin was like sunlight and bathed Narjilu in warmth, which washed through him and settled around his soul. Not to disturb her, he retreated to his watch point in the shade and guarded her through the night.

That night in the forest clearing Patience was dreamed into existence, doomed to be a halfling, one of the scullery maids of Heaven.

Narjilu felt the heat around his soul for several moons and the beautiful vision visited his dreams, but he was not one for idle thoughts, even in sleep. Out on night watch he never paused where he had first seen Rimmia, or allowed himself to wonder if she would come back. Soon his soul returned to body temperature and his dreams became solitary again.

Yet Narjilu kept time with such accuracy that he

could not ignore each anniversary of that night. Every year he felt a pang of longing as he passed the clearing, and until the moon set his soul felt cold.

Patience was not unhappy with her lot; she didn't know any different. Her mother raised her with a love as soft and sweet as a marshmallow pillow. Nevertheless she longed for something else, beyond the dazzling light and white heat of heaven. Sometimes she felt a tugging at her heartstrings so strong that she thought her heart would be dragged from her body if she resisted. But she knew nothing of her earthly roots and her unheavenly yearnings were not something she dared share with anyone, not even her mother.

Whenever Patience was unhappy, Rimmia would tell her about Earth – the wealth of creatures, the extreme landscapes, the desert, the polar icecaps, the vast forests, the oceans – but nothing about Narjilu. From childhood Rimmia had prepared Patience for her coming of age, when she would begin a life outside Heaven's kitchens, carrying blessings to Earth's people. Sometimes when she felt the mysterious tug, Patience would try to persuade herself that it was just her yearning to grow up and do some good on Earth. But on days when her heart hurt most, she didn't believe that at all and diamond tears of frustration dropped into her bucket and scratched the crystal floors as she cleaned.

Fully-fledged angels get a calling to use the gift they

were born with – heavenly chorus, messenger, cloud shaper – the list is infinite. It is different for halflings. It is rare that they know their vocation, they have to find it for themselves and forever work to be good at it. Their mortal half makes them ideal for earthly visits because they blend in, but it also makes them weaker. Once on Earth, some stay put and try to be mortal because it seems easier.

Rimmia hoped that Patience would not give up like others. But as she watched Narjilu's loneliness grow, she accepted that there might be some good in their daughter choosing mortality; though far more good would come if she chose a heavenly path.

When Patience's time came to find her gift, it was a typical winter day in between Heaven and Earth. Crisp ice crystals sparkled and a thousand suns shimmered, white gold, against the deep blue sky. Patience knew she had to go to Earth. She no longer felt the pain, just a clear sense of direction. The pull to Earth was so strong she could hardly fly, as if her body were giving in to gravity.

Rimmia came to her to say goodbye, blazing in sunshine. She stroked her daughter's hair and took her hands.

'This is your beginning,' she said and wrapped Patience in the hawthorn shawl.

'This shawl is as old as you are and the giver is very

special. You must find him and through him you will find yourself and your gift. You will know when you meet him and it will change everything.

'I cannot choose your vocation for you, Patience, but I believe you are meant to be a blessing bearer. The giver will be the first creature you bless. You may not know it at first, because that is what blessing is, an unconscious gift of love. The first is the hardest to judge and the hardest to leave behind you.'

Rimmia let go of her daughter's hand and a beam of light played between their fingers as they parted; it would join them wherever they were.

'Earth is beautiful, Patience. I know it will be hard to leave, especially for you. Try not to be blind to its imperfections. It is not Heaven, and on Earth where there is light there is always shade. Try to remember that your home is here. Try to return, whatever happens.'

Patience nodded.

'I know,' she said, even though she didn't really understand. She was feeling slightly sleepy, basking in the warmth of her mother's love. Her mother smiled at her, rather sadly she thought.

'You will understand, my love, but it's not for me to teach you everything, much as I'd like to.'

Patience was alert again, suddenly doubtful. How did her mother always know what she was thinking?

'Will I be all right?'

'Yes you will, but you must remember this journey is to find your gift and strength. Sometimes it won't be easy . . . you may find yourself weaker than you have ever been at the time you need to be strongest. But I will always be here loving you, and you will find an earthling who feels the same.'

She kissed Patience goodbye and her tears sealed like golden beads around the loose strands of Patience's hair. For a moment, Patience glowed with a radiance as bright as her mother's and they stood together in splendour. She had never felt so strong. But as soon as she left her cloud and hit the turbulence of the lower levels, she felt the clammy grey fingers of the No-Man grasping at her shawl and heard his lone murmurings in her ears, drawing her attention like a magnet.

The No-Man led a half-existence. He filled a gap between Heaven and Earth. He was lonely. If you listened to his whispers for too long, the words would take shape in your ears. They would mould themselves around your darkest fear and your greatest weakness and, as you succumbed, you would be drawn deeper into the No-Man's nothingness until you were no longer.

Patience on her cloud had no fears, but here in No-Man's Land she could hear him already,

'Shhhhhhhhhh, you're not going to maaaaaake it

. . . Aaaaaaaaaahhh, you don't belong anywheeeeeeere. Haaaaaaaah, you're not even a real aaaaaaaangel . . . Heeeeeeeere, you should stop heeeeeeeeere . . .'

Patience closed her eyes to shut out the grey and her tears. She wrapped her arms around herself to keep No-Man's chilly fingers off her heart. She could hear a tiny voice in her head saying, 'Find your strength, find your strength.'

But No-Man drowned it.

'Lisssssssssssten I'll tell you your seeeeeeeeeecret . . . Lissssssssssten, I know who you aaaaaaaare . . . Come heeeeeeeere, I'll show you the waaaaaaaay . . .'

Patience lost all sense of direction. She felt as if she were flying without moving and when she opened her eyes she could see nothing but grey. She pulled the hawthorn shawl up around her ears to shut out the No-Man's voice. The shawl's rough weave scratched her neck and a tiny ruby dropped on to her wing. She had never seen her blood before.

'What a strange present,' she thought aloud, 'that it draws blood,' and she watched the bright ruby roll off her feathers and fall into the nothingness below.

She had stopped listening to the No-Man. She now felt the familiar tug, that strange pull on her heartstrings that had caused her so much pain. Her sense of direction was back, as strong as it had been in Heaven. The Earth was calling.

As this longing took over, she felt the No-Man's grasp relax. Her heart warmed up and the air went quiet, the clouds parted and she glided into clear skies.

Suddenly she seemed to be moving at top speed again. A few cloud wisps played around her like smoke rings but they did not slow her down and before she could admire it, the Earth rushed up to meet her. Patience landed on the outskirts of a forest. The pines huddled together like old men round a card game. Single rays of sunlight played between the branches and beneath them lay long pools of shade. Patience was mesmerised, not by the light, but by the random patches of darkness between the light, dark distorting mirrors of reality. She had never seen anything so imperfect but so beautiful and her sense of belonging drew her into the forest. The branches had grown together over time and it was hard to see which trees they stemmed from.

Her sense of longing trickled away with every step. So did her sense of time and her memory of the reason for this visit. The shadows lengthened and darkness coated the forest. The soft pools of winter sun cooled and sharpened into moonshine and Patience's sense of wonder darkened too, into fear. She remembered the tales of Hell and she wondered whether, by forgetting her mission, she had strayed into the Underworld. This darkness was nothing like the clear nights of Heaven. Here she couldn't even see the ground beneath her feet.

A mist hovered below her knees and wound round her ankles like a cat. Branches tapped her on the shoulder and smothered her like hardened feather boas. She heard the giggling of night creatures drunk on sap.

Exhausted and disorientated, Patience dropped the hawthorn shawl and collapsed in the hollow of an ancient oak which stood in state, apart from the other trees. The mossy roots cradled her like arms and the rich smell of earth soothed her. Surely Hell couldn't feel so like home.

Patience slept through the pattering of weasels out poaching. She didn't hear the rhythmic thrashing of wings as Caron, the one-eyed nightmare bearer, and his troop of sleep thieves sped through the night skies looking for victims with their infra-red eyes. Cursed with insomnia for their previous ills they were only soothed by feeding on the peace of sleeping souls.

Patience dreamed she was back in No-Man's Land. She had lost the hawthorn shawl. Without it she would never get home. But she couldn't find it. Instead, she was following her sense of longing. She wandered through mist and every step she took was like missing a stair and she plummeted downwards. She could see a figure ahead of her on a parallel path, obscured by shade and she knew she was close to what she was looking for. She kept calling out but her voice was silent and the figure was ignoring her. She was being led to the mouth of Hell. It rumbled her name again and again.

Narjilu the centaur was riding through the forest on his night patrol. No longer content with their dreams, some of the forest creatures were taking to sap and firewater and marauding in the night. Narjilu had little time for these wasters. They made the winter nights seem even longer and caused him endless delays, but the peace of the dreamers was in his care.

Patience felt herself drift closer and closer to Hell's mouth. The black flames licked at her wings and her nostrils filled with the sickly smoke of her singeing feathers. As she gasped for breath, Caron hovered over her, beating the rhythm of her dream. The air was thick with his presence and his thieves swooped, sniggering behind him as he suffocated her with lies.

Narjilu was coming to the end of his rounds and to his favourite spot, the royal oak with whom he shared his dreams of right and order. Here he would spend the dawn discussing the music of the stars and the magic of sunrise. It was his haven. But as he approached a sight shot through his heart like lightning. A creature, identical to the one he had guarded endless years before, lay shivering and gasping at his feet, her face streaked with moonlit tears, a crumpled hawthorn shawl at her feet. His heart fell. This could not be the same angel that had warmed his heart. There was no trace of the sun on her skin and no peace to be had from her misery. Yet that shawl had been his dream-catcher and the sleeping angel tore from his soul a pain and longing that took his breath away.

He was a stranger to such uncontrollable emotion. He was a huntsman and a judge. He lived by forest lore and the ruthless practicalities of nature. He had seen plenty of creatures in the throes of Caron's deadly night tricks, yet here he stood frozen and blind to Caron's presence, his heart consumed with anguish and loss.

Patience was losing her strength. The heat of Hell was weakening her and her throat was tight with smoke. She was no closer to Narjilu, but her vision was clearing, as if she were hallucinating. She could see it, half man, half animal, a bow and arrow slung across its back. Clearer still she saw a tail and then to her horror, cloven feet. She had followed the Devil himself to eternal death.

A shaft of moonlight cast a black circle over the angel and Narjilu looked up to see Caron's carrion crew feasting on Patience's soul. Jolted from his paralysis Narjilu seized his bow and with a cry of fury he fired an arrow into Caron's infrared eye. As it hit home, the arrow melted into nothing, but the strength of Narjilu's anger sliced through Caron's green heart and he shrivelled around it, hissing as the last drops of bile oozed from its core.

Nothing without their leader, the sleep thieves scattered shrieking across the skies.

Their screams woke Patience. As she opened her eyes she saw the figure from her dream, bow in hand, his back to her. She was in Hell. Narjilu heard her sob. As he turned round, he saw her horror and dropped his bow, but not through fear. In her eyes he saw his own, looking back at him from an angel's face. Patience grasped at the shawl, and stared back. She knew this creature, but not from her dream. He was the gift-giver and her father.

They looked at each other, mirrors to new parts of each other's souls. While this moment lasted they belonged and neither of them dared to stir, both afraid that if they moved or spoke, their find would evaporate and they would be alone.

But Narjilu would not be conquered by fear of losing her. He believed in this beautiful vision that was partly him. He knelt down on his forelegs and held out a hand to his daughter. She took it and smiled and their hearts were locked together like the Earth and its moon.

Narjilu wrapped the hawthorn shawl around her shoulders and held her tight. She felt the salt of his tears on her skin like the sea. She smelt the earth in his hair and heard the thunder of mortal blood in his veins. They laughed and cried together in the sunrise and knew they had found the place where they were complete.

'I could stay here forever,' confessed Patience and immediately wished she hadn't. Narjilu looked at her and she lowered her eyes, overawed by his solemn gaze. Only her mother could have found her an earthling father with a heavenly sense of duty.

'You'll be back,' he smiled, 'and today we'll tour the forest so you'll always know where to find me.' As he spoke he swung her up onto his shoulders like a mortal child.

'Is this what a queen feels like?' They laughed and rode out into the dawn, knowing that even though they must part in a few Earth hours, they would never be lost from each other again.

The Best Kind of Dream

Helen Dunmore

My dad has got lots of dreams. Our house is one of them. We bought this house when I was four years old, and it didn't have a roof on it then. Friends used to say, 'At least the two of you have got a roof over your head now,' and then they'd look up and see the heavy blue tarpaulin flapping and they'd go quiet.

We have a roof now. Some of the walls have been plastered. We have a garden which contains a sink, a bath, two fireplaces, a toilet with a tree growing out of it, a heap of tyres and a jungle of bramble-bushes which are slowly swallowing up everything.

I'm used to Dad's dreams. This morning he came in all wild-haired, with a huge mug of tea in his hand to wake me up, and sat on my bed and started to tell me about how my bedroom was going to turn into paradise.

'I'm going out to get the stuff this minute. I'll give these walls a skim, I'll put lining-paper on and we can paint it any colour in the world you want.'

I asked him what giving a skim meant, and he said it was to even up the holes and lumps in my walls.

I liked the holes and lumps. They made a map, and I used to travel through it at night. But Dad was full of his dreams.

'And we'll sand that floor for you, and seal it. We'll get a rug, maybe a sheepskin. How would you like that, Saph?'

I thought about putting my bare feet down into the thick, creamy fleece of a sheepskin rug.

'Yes,' I said.

'I'll be off then. I'll bring back a colour chart, so you can choose your colours.'

'But, Dad.'

'What?'

'What about the – '

'Don't ask me about money again, Sapphire!'

Dad banged out of the room. I drank my tea.

Dad is going to get loads of money one day, quite soon. He might get it as compensation from an accident he had at work three years ago. Dad was trying to mend a photocopying machine. He had an electric shock from it which threw him across the room, and since then he's worked for himself. He has a window-cleaning business. But Dad says there's not much money in windows. People don't want to look out and see the world these days, they'd rather stare at a computer screen.

The other way Dad might make loads of money is the horses. He is brilliant at picking winners, unless he's put money on them. It's all right to say that, because Dad says it as well. If you watch a race on TV with Dad, he will point to a dull-looking horse, going steadily around the course, well back of the front-runners.

'Watch that one,' he'll say.

I watch. He's always right, unless he's put a bet on it. Up comes the dull-looking horse, on the outside, and pulls past the front-runners just before they go into the final straight.

'I *wish* you'd had a bet on it, Dad,' I'll say, and I work out how much Dad would have won if he'd had a bet on.

Thirty-three to one. Even if Dad had only put a fiver on, that would have been . . . Wow! A hundred and sixty-five pounds!

'You're forgetting the stake. I'd have got my stake back as well,' says Dad. Dad always pays his betting tax when he places his bets. It's the best way, because if you pay the tax after, it's much more.

'Your maths is coming on,' says Dad.

The third way Dad might get rich is doing up this

house. It has loads of bedrooms, because it used to be a nursing home. But then a big crack appeared in the front of the house, and all the old people moved out. Nobody lived in it for years, until we came. There were wild kittens in the bedroom, and a bush growing out of the kitchen floor. Because the roof was off, the rain had watered it.

Dad reckons our house is worth loads of money now. All he's got to do is put in a proper kitchen and bathroom, do the wiring and plumbing, finish off the roof, replace the windows, clear the garden, sort out the crack down the front of the house, put doors on the rooms that haven't got doors, and decorate everything.

'We're sitting on a goldmine, Saph!' says Dad.

I'd finished my tea by now. I climbed out of bed, and my feet hit splintery floorboards instead of a sheepskin rug. I washed in cold water (the boiler needs replacing) and went downstairs for breakfast. I knew there'd be milk in the fridge. We always have our milk delivered, because you can owe money to the milkman. The supermarket won't let you take a pint of milk and whizz through the checkout saying, 'I'll pay for it later, is that OK?'

I took my cornflakes out into the garden, and waited for Dad to come back with the colour charts. It was a beautiful sunny morning, the kind of day that always starts up Dad's dreams. I sat down on an upturned plastic milk crate that someone had thrown into our garden, and stretched out my legs into the sun. It was perfect. The cats who live under our blackberry bushes came slinking out to see if they could have the milk from my cornflakes, but I was too hungry. I promised them some milk later.

'Saph! SAPH!'

Dad was waving the colour charts at me like a fan. 'Here, take your pick.'

I picked white for the ceiling, dark blue for the wall opposite my bed, and pale blue for the other walls. The sanded floorboards would be pale gold, and my sheepskin rug would be creamy white. And maybe I'd have red curtains . . . I took a long time choosing, just as if it were all real.

'It's a bit late to go to the shops now,' said Dad. 'I'll go tomorrow, and get everything we need. Paint-brushes, rollers – the lot. Wait till your friends see it.'

My friends like my room the way it is. Or if they don't, then they aren't my friends. When I have sleepovers I always boil up loads of water in the morning so they can have a proper wash. They like having breakfast in the garden. They like the cats.

'Yeah, we'll get it tomorrow, Dad,' I said. The sun was moving to another part of the garden, so I moved, too. Dad was staring at the corner of the garden where the old bath lay full of weeds.

'A couple of rose-bushes would be lovely there,' he said. 'Like a rose arbour.'

The next day, Dad didn't go and buy the stuff to decorate my room. I knew he wouldn't, so I didn't get disappointed.

'I'll go on Monday,' he said, 'to that new superstore on the other side of town. We could make a day of it. Do you fancy a day off school, Saph?'

'OK,' I said.

We were walking down to the shops late that day.

'Got any spare change?' asked a man sitting on the ground with his dog. Dad felt in his pockets and brought out some change. He picked out a twenty pence piece and a ten pence piece, and put them into the man's hand. Dad never just throws coins into the cup.

I couldn't help it, I said out loud, 'Why did you give him all that, Dad?'

'He needs it, poor fella.'

'So do we.'

'Saph, he's not even got a roof over his head.'

I was so angry.

'Maybe he has,' I said. 'You don't know. Maybe he's saving up to decorate his daughter's bedroom.'

Dad looked at me. His eyes seemed to want to hide inside his head. 'Is that what you think of me, Saph?'

'No, Dad, I didn't mean it, it was only –'

But Dad was gone. He was striding away down the

pavement, almost running. I bought the loaf of bread we'd come for, and went back to the house, to wait for Dad.

I waited a long time. I had my tea in the garden, then I fed the cats and came in. I watched TV. We have a black-and-white TV, which Dad says doesn't count, so we don't have to have a TV licence. All the same I have a special place for it under the blackberry bushes, for when the TV detector van is around.

I ate a peanut butter sandwich, and drank some more milk. I made a card for Dad, and I propped it up on the kitchen table and went to bed. But even travelling across the map of holes and lumps on my wall couldn't make me sleep.

I must have slept in the end, because Dad woke me when he put his key in the front door. I was over the floorboards and down the stairs in a second.

'Saph.' He looked up at me from under the hall light bulb. I could see how wild his hair was, and how tired his face.

'I'm sorry, Dad.'

'Come on down and see something.'

I went down and we sat at the kitchen table. Dad slid a hand into his pocket. He brought out a brown envelope and laid it flat on the table.

'Open it up, Saph.'

I took hold of the envelope. It weighed heavy. I

glanced at Dad but he didn't look excited, or even interested. He didn't look as if he'd had a dream this time.

I drew out a slab of clean, new notes. They were ten pound notes. I stroked their edges apart, and all the notes were all the same.

'Count them,' said Dad. 'There should be five hundred pounds there. Enough to do your room.'

I laid the money on the table without counting it. Had Dad won the money on the horses? No, if he had money on it the horse would fall, or have to be pulled up. Had someone lent him the money? No, we didn't know anyone who would lend us five hundred pounds. Had he begged for it? No, it was all new clean notes. No one would drop that much money in a cup. So where had it come from?

'We'll be able to get you the rug as well,' said Dad. But the dream had gone from his voice.

'It's not our money, is it?' I asked.

'Yes, it's our money.'

I was trying to work out how many windows Dad would have had to clean to get this much money, but my maths wasn't good enough this time.

'It's family money,' said Dad.

'What family?'

'Your family.'

'But you're my family.'

'Your grandmother.'

'I haven't got a –' But I stopped, because of course it wasn't true. My grandmother didn't see us, but she was always there. She blames my dad, because of what happened to my mum. If it hadn't been for him, Mum would never have had to go into hospital. She would never have had to live the way she does. But Dad had always told me it wasn't true, what my grandmother said. My mum has an illness in her mind which means she needs to live where doctors can look after her. *Some people get it, but you never will, Saph,* he told me. My grandmother had wanted to take me, when my mum first went into hospital. My grandmother had said that Dad wasn't fit to look after me.

'But you were,' I always said, when it came to that part of the story.

Dad sat at the kitchen table and looked at me.

'I went to see her,' said Dad. 'I told her about your room. I told her I couldn't afford to do it for you. So she went down to the building society and took out some of her savings. She wants you to write to her. That'll be to make sure you've got the money.'

I stared at the money, and then at Dad. I knew he didn't like my grandmother. I didn't know if I liked her or not. I could remember her, but I hadn't seen her for years.

'Was she – was she, you know, all right about it?' I asked.

'What do you think, Saph?'

I knew that my grandmother had made Dad feel terrible.

'I don't want my bedroom done,' I said.

'You've got to have it now.'

As I lay in my bed that night, the streetlight shone through the curtains and I looked at the map on my wall, but I didn't know where I was going. After a long time I heard Dad coming upstairs. I listened to the sounds of Dad getting ready for bed, but I still lay awake. I was thinking about Dad's dreams. I thought about the horses and lottery tickets, and the compensation from work, and all the magic ways of making money. I thought of the five hundred pounds in the brown envelope, and how terrible Dad had looked. He had the money to do my room, but he looked as if his dream was gone. I wondered what my grandmother had said to him.

'You're not fit to look after her, are you?'

I thought about the blue tarpaulin, and the TV under the blackberry bushes, and how nice it was eating cornflakes in the sun with the cats. We always had fresh milk. And there wasn't a single other person in my class whose house had six bedrooms.

I swung my feet over the side of the bed. I tiptoed

across the floorboards, and opened my door without a creak. I trod lightly down the stairs and into the kitchen. The envelope was still on the table, as I knew it would be. Dad never bothers about putting things away.

I wrapped the brown envelope in an old newspaper. I emptied out the bin, put the envelope wrapped in newspaper in the bottom of it, and filled the bin up again with old teabags and empty baked bean tins. Then I swept the floor and washed my hands. One of the cats came in and wrapped itself round my legs, purring. I tiptoed back upstairs, lay down and went straight to sleep.

In the morning I heard Dad banging and thumping about downstairs. I knew what he was looking for. I lay still, and pretended to sleep. His feet came rushing up the stairs and he burst into the room.

'Saph! Have you seen that envelope?'

Of course I hadn't. No one could see it. It was invisible at the bottom of the bin.

'It's gone,' I said.

'What do you mean?'

'The cats got it. The rain came in through the roof and washed it away.'

'Did it rain last night?'

'I don't know. I was asleep.'

'Saph – '

'It's all right, Dad. It was just a dream. A bad dream. We never had that envelope at all.'

'Didn't we?'

'No.'

I rolled over and looked at the map on the wall. 'Anyway, I don't want to change my room,' I said. 'I like it the way it is.'

'Do you, Saph? Do you really?'

'Yeah. Besides, we can always paint it one day, if we want to.'

'Any colour you like, Saph,' said Dad.

'Have we got some milk for cornflakes, Dad? I'm starving.'

Dad leapt up off the bed and bounded to the door. 'Of course we have! There's always pints of the stuff in the fridge.'

I thought of the money in the bin. Maybe I should have kept back just one ten pound note, to pay the milkman . . .

The Authors

Anne Fine is a distinguished writer for children of all ages, with over forty books to her credit. She is the current Children's Laureate, twice winner of the Carnegie Medal, and has also won the Guardian Children's Literature Award, the Whitbread Children's Book Award twice, and the Smarties Prize. Twentieth Century Fox filmed her novel *Madame Doubtfire*, starring Robin Williams. Her books include *Bill's New Frock*, *Goggle-Eyes* and *The Tulip Touch*.

'My own father had to divide what attention he had to offer between my mother, myself and my four sisters. So it came as a real surprise to me when my own two daughters came to respond to their own dad – especially after the divorce – not simply as a man in a role, but as a real human being with his own passions and interests and convictions.

'What's interesting now is that, though they're more than old enough to get exasperated with just being "mothered" by me, they still take a tremendous interest in all the things they once had to learn to share with him.

'But that's family, isn't it? Swings and roundabouts, always. And actually, I find that tremendously cheering.'

Marilyn McLaughlin is the award-winning author of the hugely popular *Fierce Milly* stories, the first of which won a Bisto Award and The Eilís Dillon Award for best first book for children in 2000. She has also published a collection of stories for adults, *A Dream Woke Me*.

'I wrote this story for my father who died suddenly when I was nineteen. As his daughter all I had ever known of him was his bigness, his unfailing kindness, his humour, his story-telling, and the sense of utter safety and being "looked after" that the mere sight of him brought. I especially remember his hands. I have inherited them: squarish, capable hands. He took us out into the big waves, walked us along cliff paths and let us fish in deep water, but we always knew we were in safe hands, hands that knew when to hold and, more importantly, when to let go. He was an uncomplicated and sweet-natured person. I shall miss him for ever.'

Adèle Geras, a full-time writer since 1976, has been published all over the world. In the USA she has won The Sydney Taylor Award for *My Grandmother's Stories* (1991) and The National Jewish Book Award for *Golden Windows* (1994). She has also won prizes for her adult poetry and her most recent children's novel, *Troy*, was highly commended for the Carnegie Medal, the Whitbread and the Guardian Children's Book Award.

'My dad was nothing like the father in this story. He was completely useless in the kitchen and round the house, but he was perfect as a teacher and companion. He introduced me to all sorts of poets at a very early age, and took me round art galleries and bought me lots of lovely postcards of the paintings, which I stuck into an exercise book. He talked to me all the time as though I were his age: a friend of his, rather than his daughter. It's sad that he died before I became a writer . . . he'd have loved the whole business and he'd have read everything very carefully. To this day, because of him, I would NEVER split an infinitive nor say "under the circumstances" because he taught me that "in the circumstances" was correct. I have inherited from him my shortsightedness, my laziness and any talent I have as a writer.

'Fathers don't figure very much as main characters in my books, but I am very fond of the Singer in my novel *Troy*, who is a sort of grandfather figure. I must put my own dad in a story some day . . .'

Jacqueline Wilson has been a writer since she was seventeen and has had over sixty books published. She is twice winner of the Guardian Children's Book Award and the Smarties Prize, with three of her books shortlisted for the Carnegie Medal. Her books include *The Illustrated Mum*, *The Story of Tracy Beaker* and *Vicky Angel*.

'I'm always very pleased and proud when Miriam Hodgson invites me to contribute to her anthologies – but I hesitated this time when she told me she wanted a short story with a father/daughter theme. I didn't have a comfortable relationship with my own father. I've always felt very wistful when I see dads making a huge fuss of their daughters. The dads are often missing in my books! The father fails to make a vital appearance in "The Most Wonderful Father in the World", but I think he still manages to be a very important character all the same. My own father certainly wasn't wonderful but I was very happy that he managed to be a much-loved grandpa to my daughter Emma before he died.'

The Authors

Julie Bertagna is the author of *The Spark Gap* and the highly acclaimed *Soundtrack*, which won the Scottish Arts Council Children's Book Award. *Dolphin Boy* was shortlisted for the NASEN Special Needs and the Blue Peter Book Awards. *The Ice Cream Machine* is being developed for TV. Scottish Book Trust published her essay, "Towards a Creative Nation", to mark the opening of the Scottish Parliament and the National Year of Reading in 1999.

'The red armchair that sits at the end of the airport runway is real. I spotted it one Saturday afternoon when I went along with my partner and young daughter on one of their plane-spotting trips to Glasgow airport. There were lots of other dads there with their children, picnicking as they watched the planes take off right overhead. It seemed like one of those special things kids do with their dad, something they would always remember. I found myself looking at the dilapidated red armchair at the runway fence, wondering about it. My dad died not so long ago, so when I came to write this story somehow the red chair and all the plane-spotting dads with their children merged with my own feelings and memories. The scene in the car is true and what my dad said to me then has influenced me all through my life. So although it's a story about loss, it ends with a strong sense that some part of a father lives on in his daughter.'

Steve May has had many plays broadcast on BBC Radio and has won prizes for his poetry and television drama. Of his novels for children, *Dazzer Plays On* featured in the Daily Telegraph's Best 10 Reads of 2000. His other books include *Egghead, Friendly Fire* and *Is That Your Dog?*

'My daughter, I think she's great. Before she was born, I foolishly imagined I wanted a son. Sons are fun, but they don't stretch you like daughters. My daughter brings out the best and the worst in me: I'll wade through burning cornflakes to help her, but when I get there I can't resist giving her Good Advice (that means telling her what to do). All the stupid things the two fathers say in my story are things I've said, or fathers I know. Sad lot, aren't we? But, I hope we'll always come running when the cornflakes catch fire.

'P.S. Shhh, daughter back from abroad where she now lives, read this, called it cheesy. Said I'd change it. Haven't. Sorry.'

Stephen Potts' novel *Compass Murphy* was shortlisted for the Askew's Book Award, while *Hunting Gumnor* (shortlisted for the Branford Boase award for first novels) and *Tommy Trouble* both received nominations for the Carnegie Medal.

'There are many different threads in the complicated cord that binds fathers and daughters together. These stories pick away at that cord, teasing out and highlighting some of the filaments and fibres. One such is the tension between *want* and *need*. "Abigail's Gift" is about a father who works himself numb to provide the material things he thinks his family have to have; and a daughter who see he has got it wrong, and seeks to protect him from his mistake. There is a bike she wants, but she knows that what she and her family need is not nearly so solid or so shiny, and much harder to find: Time Spent Together. So she sets out to capture some.

'In my first book, *Hunting Gumnor*, I've written about a different daughter and a different dad, whose cord is made of Other Stuff – but is no less strong. They begin by desperately wanting the same thing – the return of the strange sea-beast they care for – but even while their shared search binds them together, life pulls them in different directions, as if to unsplice them.'

Elinor Hodgson published her first story, "Through the Looking Glass", in an anthology called *Allnighter*, in 1997. Since then she has combined writing with being Managing Editor of an antiquarian and rare book site, worldbookdealers.com, and studying for an MA in the History of the Book.

'I wrote this story for my father. A good father daughter relationship is a boundless treasure. Words may not do it justice, but we must try to describe it, so others can share and recognize its joys – and cherish it.'

Helen Dunmore is the author of the delightful *Allie* stories for younger children. She is also a poet and a very successful writer of novels for adults; she was the winner of the first Orange Prize in 1996 for *A Spell of Winter*, and her other work includes *Your Blue-Eyed Boy* and the highly acclaimed *The Siege*.

'The love between fathers and daughters has been celebrated for centuries in stories, films, songs and poems. It's a mix of protection, tenderness, support, rebellion, loyalty, shared jokes and a million other emotions. Close your eyes and think of dads and daughters, and see what comes to mind . . .

'. . . Dads going out on cold nights to give daughters a lift home, daughters telling dads that they've got to throw away that old jacket, dads yelling, daughters running to their rooms and slamming the door, dads crouched in tiny chairs to talk to teachers on parents' evenings, daughters bringing home Father's Day cards covered in glitter, hearts and kisses, dads carrying their daughters' photos in their wallets, daughters showing dads how to do stuff on the computer, dads dancing embarrassingly at their daughters' birthday discos . . .

'Many fathers and daughters live apart, even when they would prefer to be together. Other fathers take on the job of bringing up their children alone. I chose to write about a daughter who lives alone with her father. There isn't much money, the roof leaks and the garden is full of cats, rubbish and sunshine. Saph loves her father dearly – but sometimes he drives her crazy . . .'